"Look, I've already called the police," Frankie lied, "so if I were you, I'd just leave."

"You would?" Arlo's cool dark gaze made breathing a challenge. "But things are just starting to get interesting." She tugged the quilt more tightly around her body as he looked down at her. "In fact, you should probably give the police a call back. Ask them to bring a ball. Then we could actually make use of that bat you're waving around so enthusiastically."

What?

Frankie looked at him in confusion.

She could count the number of conversations she'd had with burglars on one finger, but surely this wasn't how they were supposed to go.

"Do you think this is funny?" she snapped.

"No, I don't." His gaze bored into her. "Do you?"

"Of course not—"

"In that case—" he paused, his eyes narrowing on her face with such a mixture of exasperation and hostility that she had to look away "—do you think it would be too much trouble to tell me exactly what you're doing in *my* bed?"

Louise Fuller was a tomboy who hated pink and always wanted to be the prince—not the princess! Now she enjoys creating heroines who aren't pretty pushovers but are strong, believable women. Before writing for Harlequin, she studied literature and philosophy at university, then worked as a reporter on her local newspaper. She lives in Royal Tunbridge Wells with her impossibly handsome husband, Patrick, and their six children.

Books by Louise Fuller

Harlequin Presents

Craving His Forbidden Innocent
The Rules of His Baby Bargain
The Man She Should Have Married
Italian's Scandalous Marriage Plan

Secret Heirs of Billionaires

Kidnapped for the Tycoon's Baby
Demanding His Secret Son
Proof of Their One-Night Passion

The Sicilian Marriage Pact

The Terms of the Sicilian's Marriage

Visit the Author Profile page
at Harlequin.com for more titles.

Louise Fuller

BEAUTY IN THE BILLIONAIRE'S BED

HARLEQUIN
PRESENTS

HARLEQUIN®
PRESENTS®

Recycling programs
for this product may
not exist in your area.

ISBN-13: 978-1-335-56896-0

Beauty in the Billionaire's Bed

Harlequin Enterprises ULC
22 Adelaide St. West, 40th Floor
Toronto, Ontario M5H 4E3, Canada
www.Harlequin.com

Printed in U.S.A.

BEAUTY IN THE BILLIONAIRE'S BED

To Larry, Leonard, Neil and Neville.
For forcing me into the fresh air and
occasionally bringing clarity to my thoughts.

CHAPTER ONE

THE TRAIN BURST out of the tunnel into the fading light. Frankie Fox flinched as the carriage jerked sideways.

It had taken just over two years of persistence and hard work, but finally it had happened. Two days ago her social media profile—@StoneCold-RedHotFox—had reached the milestone of a million followers.

Better still, the man of her dreams had invited her to spend the weekend at Hadfield Hall, his family's home in Northumberland.

She should have been feeling on cloud nine, but instead she was staring morosely through the grimy window at a darkening landscape.

It was her fault she was feeling this way.

For the first time in two years she had let herself dream, let herself hope that she might be given a second chance to belong. That maybe she had done enough to earn a place in someone's life.

And the day had started so promisingly...

After weeks of rain, she had woken up to a pale March sun in a sky of clear harebell-blue.

Miraculously, she had got to the station with time to spare and, best of all, Johnny had been waiting beneath the clock, just as he'd said he would be.

They'd met just shy of three months ago at a product launch. Technically, she had been working, but that had been quickly forgotten because for her it had been love at first sight.

Johnny Milburn was an actor—the kind described as 'hot' and 'up-and-coming'. He certainly looked like a leading man, with that lean body and clean-cut superhero features, the floppy blond hair, a smile that could power the National Grid, and the most beautiful meltingly soft chocolate-coloured eyes.

She had been the one melting when he'd taken her hands last Saturday and told her that she was working too hard. That somebody had to tell her she needed a break, and that person was him.

She breathed out unsteadily, remembering how his eyes had been fixed on her face as if there was nobody in the world but her. He hadn't kissed her, but incredibly—unbelievably—he had invited her to spend the weekend with him at Hadfield Hall, his family's estate on a tidal island off the coast of Northumberland. It had all sounded swooningly romantic. Like something out of a Georgette Heyer novel…

She glanced across the table to where Johnny *should* have been sitting.

Except romantic novels needed a hero and a heroine, and right now her hero was somewhere over the Atlantic on his way to an audition in Los Angeles, and she was on her way to Northumberland alone.

Slumping back in her seat, she sighed.

She'd tried telling Johnny that she couldn't possibly just turn up at his family's house on her own, but he wouldn't listen to her.

'Please, Frankie. It's bad enough that I can't go, but if you don't go either then I might as well call off the trip to LA, because I won't be able to stop thinking about how I messed everything up for you.'

'But what am I supposed to say to your brother?' she'd asked.

Remembering how Johnny's expression had changed from pleading to relief, she let her head fall against the train window. She'd been trying to make him see the impracticality of what he was suggesting, but instead she had simply given him the means to make refusing impossible.

'Arlo?' He'd frowned. 'You won't have to say anything to him. I thought he was home, but apparently he's on some ice floe in the Antarctic. He probably won't be back for months.'

That at least was something, she thought, gazing up at the rain-spattered glass.

Johnny's brother, Arlo Milburn, was not just a decorated former marine and a renowned expert on all things environmental, he was also a polar explorer. She had been dreading meeting him with Johnny there, but doing so on her own—

She shivered.

It was just lucky for her that he was away, because guilt had made Johnny unusually single-minded.

'Look, it's perfect for you.' He'd held up his phone to show her. 'For starters, it's basically off-grid. Plus, you can have the run of the place. Nobody will be there except Constance—'

'Who's Constance?'

He'd frowned. 'She looks after the house.'

'Won't she think it a bit odd, me just turning up on my own?'

'No,' Johnny had said firmly. 'She hates it when Arlo's away. Honestly, she'll love having you there. And you'll love it too. It'll be like a home from home.' He'd taken her hand and squeezed it. 'Besides, I've already called her and left a message saying you're coming, so you *have* to go now, Frankie.'

He'd been so racked with remorse, so contrite, so very handsome...

And, anyway, what would the alternative have been? Running home with her tail between her legs?

It was getting dark now outside, and for a moment she stared at her reflection.

And then what?

If she went out then she would have to pretend

everything was fine, and she just didn't have the energy to do that. But if she stayed in then she would be alone with her thoughts...

No, with or without Johnny, she needed a break—a change of scene. A few days away in Northumberland was exactly what the doctor ordered.

Suddenly her heart was racing, and even though she could feel her hands, could see the jutting bleached-out knobs of her knuckles, it felt as though she was losing substance.

Of course the opposite was true.

She alone had survived.

Her shoulders jerked. Even now it was a physical pain. Knowing that everyone she loved, everyone who had loved her, was gone.

Her family had been coming back from a summer holiday in Provence. Her father had been flying the plane when it had crashed. The crash had killed him, her mother, and her twin brother and sister.

She alone had survived.

And every day she wondered why.

'This train will shortly be arriving at Berwick-upon-Tweed.'

The automated voice broke into her thoughts as she fought for calm.

'Please remember to take all your belongings with you before you leave the train.'

Her fingers tightened on the armrest. After the

shock had worn off there had been endless paper-work to fill in, meetings with solicitors, and then finally the inquest.

A shiver ran over her skin.

She had told the truth, but nothing she'd said had made any difference. That was when she'd started blogging and she hadn't stopped since. But working non-stop for eighteen months had taken its toll. She was sleeping badly, had trouble con-centrating, and lately she had a strange, disquiet-ing feeling of being erased…like a drawing that wasn't quite good enough—

Jolted back into the present, and glancing around, she saw that the carriage was empty. Standing up, she pulled her suitcase down from the overhead luggage rack.

Everything would be fine. Once she reached the Hall, she could relax and unwind. And if she felt like doing something more strenuous she could go for a walk along the beach or just do some cloud-spotting.

And there were plenty of clouds to spot, she thought twenty minutes later, as she hugged her beautiful but utterly ineffective quilted jacket around her shivering body. In fact, the sky was pretty much one huge, dark cloud, and the half-hearted rain from earlier was now sheeting down in force as she rapped on the door with the huge cast-iron knocker.

She waited, squinting up at the immense grey stone house rising above her, her heart beating in time to the raindrops hitting her face.

In her head, she'd imagined Constance opening the door, smiling warmly. But there was no sign of any housekeeper, with or without a smile, and all the windows looked ominously dark...

Trying to still the jittery feeling in her legs, she pulled out her phone. Perhaps she should call Johnny.

No service.

She bit her lip. So did that mean Constance had never got Johnny's message about her coming alone?

Turning, she felt a quiver of apprehension scamper down her backbone as she watched the tail-lights of the taxi she'd hired at the station disappear into the rain.

There was no way she was walking back over that cobbled causeway in this weather. And it wasn't as if she would be breaking in or anything...

Turning her back against the thundering rain, she found the key Johnny had given her, pushed it into the lock, and turned it.

It was toe-curlingly dark inside. Her heart thudding, she fumbled for a light switch.

Oh, wow.

She was standing in a tennis-court-sized entrance hall. Water was dripping down her legs into her trainers, but she was too distracted to care.

Home from home, Johnny had said. Clearly that depended on your definition of 'home', she thought, gazing up at the huge mahogany staircase, the stucco ceiling, and innumerable gold-framed oil paintings on the walls.

She had known Johnny came from money. Not the professionally earned sort, but old money—the kind that came with a small but exclusive circle of acquaintances, a flat in Eaton Square, and a country estate. She knew, too, that he had a cousin who was a lord or an earl or something.

Only she had never really put it into context until now.

Her stomach twisted. What would it be like to live here? To be the lady of the house? But of course ordinary people like her didn't actually *live* in places like this. At most they stayed for a weekend—or, in her case, one night.

Tomorrow she would pay whatever it cost to take a taxi to the nearest hotel. Johnny would understand.

Her heart leapt in her throat as a noisy cluster of raindrops hit the windows.

Maybe in the morning she might take a quick peek around the house. Right now, though, she just wanted to go to bed.

Upstairs, there was an unbelievable number of bedrooms, all awash with heavy fabrics and

Persian rugs and paintings of horses. Feeling like Goldilocks, she wandered from one room to another, pressing her hand against the velvet bedspreads to test the mattresses.

That one was too soft, this one was too hard, but this one...

Like all the other rooms, this one was large, but it had a different feel to it. There was an overflowing bookcase, a battered trunk at the end of the bed, and a large shabby wicker dog basket beneath the window.

The mattress dipped as she sat down on the edge of the mahogany-framed four-poster bed.

This one was just right.

She washed her face and brushed her teeth in the large and very austere en suite bathroom. No toiletries. Just dark grey tiles, a bath the size of a boat, and a leather armchair that looked like something from a gentlemen's club.

Oh, and a cricket bat leaning incongruously against the wall, as if someone had just walked in off the pitch.

She stared at it in silence, frowning, and then picked it up. She might be on an island, in a house that looked as if it had been built to keep out invaders from across the sea, but it wouldn't hurt to have a little extra protection to hand.

Back in the bedroom, she peeled off her damp clothes and reached into her suitcase for the old dress shirt of her dad's that she wore to bed.

Instead her hand brushed against something seductively soft and she pulled out the whisper of midnight-blue silk she had packed, in case 'something happened' with Johnny.

Her breath caught in her throat as she remembered the moment when she'd seen it in the shop.

She'd wanted to look cool and confident and sexy. That was who she was, after all. A stone-cold, red-hot fox. Or at least it was who she was pretending to be. In reality, she felt anything but.

Throat tightening, she closed her fingers around the flimsy fabric.

She might as well wear it. Who knew when— *if*—she would have an opportunity to do so again?

Wriggling under the quilt, she gazed up at the heavy draped tapestry curtains. She felt as if she was in a fairy tale. If only Johnny were here with her, it would be perfect.

But he wasn't.

Grabbing one of the pillows, she hugged it close to her body.

Life was not a fairy tale—at least not *her* life, anyway. And her supposed prince would be on the other side of the ocean by now.

Reaching over, she switched off the light.

Instantly the empty house creaked into life. Pipes hummed, windows rattled, and there was a distant thump like a door slamming.

Rolling onto her side, she yawned. The sound of the rain was making her feel sleepy...

And then she heard it. The sound of footsteps.

She sat upright so fast she thought her spine would snap. Her pulse was racing, her heartbeat bouncing off the walls.

It's just your imagination, she told herself, feeling the hairs on the back of her neck stand up.

Except the footsteps were getting closer.

Her ears pricked, she groped frantically in the darkness for the cricket bat—and then almost jerked out of her skin when the door clicked open.

'What the—?'

There was a crash, and then a thump, as someone—*no*, not someone...a man—collided with something solid in the darkness and she heard him swear explosively.

She felt a jolt of panic. Her heart was thumping uncontrollably, her fear so intense that she was shivering all over, and then sudden light blinded her.

Blinking, she stared across the room.

Her suitcase was lying on its back, rocking from side to side like an upended turtle. A man was standing next to it, his huge shoulders filling the doorway, his face shrouded beneath a hood, a bulky-looking dark leather bag in his hand and a dog quivering beside him.

Terror doused her like a bucket of cold water as he dropped the bag and took a step forward. Edging back against the headboard, she held the cricket bat out threateningly in front of her, tension bunching her muscles.

'Don't come any closer,' she managed.

There was a silence, and then the man reached up and pushed back the hood. Eyes the colour of the storm clouds outside locked onto hers.

'Or what?'

His voice sounded as if it was rolling across shingle.

'Come closer and you'll find out,' she said hoarsely.

He leaned almost casually against the doorjamb, his lips twisting into something halfway between a smile and a sneer, so that she caught a glimpse of straight white teeth.

'Is that an invitation?'

She felt goosebumps erupt over her skin.

An invitation!

Shocked, she gazed up at him, open-mouthed.

Not in a million years was her first response.

He was tall, and even though she couldn't see beneath the bulky jacket he was wearing there was a sense of restrained power beneath the almost languid pose. But she liked her men pretty, and this man was not pretty. In fact, his features were strikingly discordant—part-Modigliani, part-Picasso, part-Border Reiver.

He had a too-big mouth, surrounded by a dark, scruffy moustache and beard. His broad nose looked as if it had been broken at some time, maybe several times, in the past, and there was a scar cutting across his left cheek like the cleft in a peach.

Maybe if they had met under other circumstances, when she was feeling more generous, she might have described him as 'unconventionally handsome'. But, given that he had just broken into the house where she was staying and scared her half to death, she wasn't feeling generous.

And yet...

There was something compelling about him— an uncompromising, unapologetic, raw masculinity that felt real in a way that both shocked and excited her. She could almost imagine him standing on the island's clifftops, his grey eyes narrowed on the foam-flecked sea ...

Blinking out of this train of thought, she glared at him hot-cheeked, her fingers tightening around the handle of the cricket bat.

'Look, I've already called the police,' she lied. 'So if I were you, I'd just leave.'

'You would?'

His cool, dark gaze made breathing a challenge. 'But things are just starting to get interesting...'

She tugged the quilt more tightly around her body as he looked down at her.

'In fact, you should probably give the police a call back. Ask them to bring a ball. Then we can actually make use of that bat you're waving around so enthusiastically.'

What?

Frankie looked at him in confusion. She could count the number of conversations she'd had with burglars on one finger, but surely this wasn't how they were supposed to go.

'Do you think this is funny?' she snapped.

'No, I don't.' His gaze bored into her. 'Do you?'

'Of course not—'

'In that case…' He paused, his eyes narrowing on her face with such a mixture of exasperation and hostility that she had to look away. 'Do you think it would be too much trouble to tell me exactly what you're doing in *my* bed?'

Frankie's head jerked up. She stared at him, her pulse doing some kind of complicated step-ball-change.

His bed.

Her eyes dropped to the bag by his feet—more specifically to the initials embossed on the leather.

A. M.

A.M.

In other words, Arlo Milburn…

She groaned inwardly as a grainy silence filled the room. 'Wh-what are you doing here?' she finally stammered. 'You're not supposed to be here.'

Shifting his weight away from the doorframe, he walked slowly across the room, stopping at the end of the bed.

'I think you'll find that's *my* line,' he said coldly.

* * *

Watching the woman's pale face stiffen with shock and panic, Arlo Milburn felt his jaw tighten. The last few days had been some of the most stressful and frustrating in his life.

He'd been on his way from the research station on the Brunt Ice Shelf to speak at a climate conference in Nairobi. It was an important conference. They all were. But when they'd landed at Durban one of the engineers had spotted an electrical fault on the plane, so instead he'd spent eight hours pacing the hangar, missing his connecting flight and his chance to speak.

And then, as if that wasn't bad enough, Emma—his extremely efficient assistant—had called to tell him that she had broken her arm and was going to be off work for at least six weeks.

Thwarted at every turn, he'd randomly decided to come home.

Big mistake.

Thanks to the frenetic arrival of Storm Delia on British shores, his journey had been plagued with even more delays. He was cold, wet, and tired, and he wanted to go to bed.

Only his bed was already taken.

By some unknown female who looked as if she had stepped out of that painting by Titian in the entrance hall. Except she was wielding a cricket bat.

Arlo scowled. 'Well? Why are you here? In my house? In my bed? And make it quick—otherwise *I* will call the police, and unlike you I won't be bluffing.'

He felt a rush of gratification as a faint flush of colour spread over her cheeks.

'Stop interrogating me like some sergeant-major,' she snapped. 'You're not in the army now.'

His gaze narrowed. 'I never was. I was a marine. That's the navy. And I was a captain, not a sergeant-major.'

She gave him a withering look. 'Fine...whatever. I thought Johnny had spoken to you.' She bit her lip, doing a good impression of confusion and dismay. 'He said he'd called you.'

Johnny. But of course—

Arlo's jaw clenched and he swore under his breath, wondering what else his brother had told this woman. He'd been taking care of Johnny ever since their grief-stricken father had retreated to his artist's studio after their mother died, and he loved him unconditionally. But his brother was not without his flaws.

Poor timekeeping. A failure to do what he said he would do. And, last but not least, his refusal to judge a book by its cover—something this scheming little redhead had clearly spotted and mined to her advantage.

'Where is he?' he demanded.

She blinked; her mouth was trembling. 'I don't know exactly.'

Her eyes locked on his, and for a split second he

forgot his anger, forgot that he was cold and tired. Instead, he stared at her mutely, held captive by the blue of those eyes.

It was the same blue as an Antarctic summer sky. The kind of blue that almost verged on purple, like the flowers on the fragrant, woody rosemary that grew so abundantly in the Hall's kitchen garden.

Maybe that was why he was having to dig his heels into the faded Afghan carpet to stop himself from leaning over and inhaling her scent.

His breath hitched. Johnny was never without a woman in his life. As soon as he'd become a teenager a constant stream of interchangeable leggy girls had started trailing after him, and that hadn't changed as an adult. But for some reason the idea of his little brother and this particular woman put his back up.

Probably because she was an impudent little madam who had no doubt been bowling men over with that look her entire life.

Not him, though.

His back straightened. 'Look, I've spent the last two days in trains, planes, and taxis. I'm cold and tired and I nearly broke my neck tripping over your damn case, so I'm really not in the mood for a game of hide and seek.'

Her chin jerked up and he knew he was doing a poor job of hiding his frustration—which, of course, only made him more frustrated.

'I'm not playing games. Johnny's not here, he's—' she began, her red curls bouncing in indignation, but he cut her off.

'What do you mean, he's not here? If you're here, he has to be here.' Glancing down, he noticed a lumpy shape beneath the bedding and his temper flared. 'What the—?'

The woman scrambled up the bed as he jerked the quilt free of her hands. 'Are you crazy? What are you doing?'

Arlo gazed down at the pillow, and then back at the woman, and a bolt of heat exploded in his groin. The shock of finding her in his bed had blinded him to all but the most obvious features of her appearance, so that he'd registered nothing much more than those eyes, a lot of freckles, and that hair. Now, though, he was registering a lot more.

His eyes skimmed over her near-naked body.

A whole lot more.

She was wearing some kind of dark blue silky slip. Yes, *slip* was the right word for it, he thought, his heart pounding like a cannon against his ribcage. He felt as though the floor had turned to ice and he was sliding sideways.

Her skin was pale, and he knew it would be stupidly smooth to the touch, but it was what was hinted at beneath the slip that was that was making his body ache. The press of her nipples, the provocative curve of her bottom…

He closed his eyes briefly to compose himself, and then tossed the bedding back towards her. 'He's not here.'

'I just told you that,' she said hotly. 'We were supposed to come up here together, only then he got called back for a part and he had to fly out to LA. Anyway, he gave me a key and told me I could have the run of the place.'

'Did he?' He raised an eyebrow. 'How very generous of him.' He saw her teeth clench.

'He didn't know you were going to be here. He was just trying to do a nice thing for me.'

She left the sentence there, but it was clear from the curl of her lip that she considered such 'niceness' beyond Arlo.

'And you are...?' he said impatiently.

'Frankie Fox.'

What kind of a name was that?

A rush of exasperation collided with a sharp, intense desire to press his mouth against hers and wipe that impudent curl from her lips.

'Hence the hair, I suppose?' He stared at her witheringly. 'Do you change your name when you dye it a different colour?'

'This *is* my hair colour.' Her eyes flashed with undisguised irritation. 'And my name is the one my parents gave me.'

Tilting his head to one side, he sighed. 'I'm guessing you're an actor too. They usually are... Johnny's fangirls.'

He'd wanted to cut her down to size only watching the way she wrapped her arms around herself, as if she was cold, he suddenly felt something pinch inside him.

But it wasn't as if Johnny could be serious about her. Sure, she was pretty, but his brother was swimming in beautiful women.

Her chin jutted forward. 'I'm not an actor,' she said stiffly. 'I'm a social media influencer.'

He frowned. 'A what?'

He knew what social media was, but an influencer...?

'A. Social. Media. Influencer.'

She was speaking each word slowly, as if English wasn't his first language or he was hard of hearing.

'Basically, brands send me clothes and accessories and I get paid to tell my followers about them.'

By 'followers' he supposed she meant a bunch of young men with their tongues hanging out.

'Sounds *fascinating.*'

As payback for the eye-roll that had accompanied her reply, he deliberately made no effort to hide the derision in his voice. His eyes bored into the quilt she was clutching to her chest, then shifted to the thin satin straps hugging her shoulders.

'So who exactly are you expecting to "influence" dressed like that?'

The question ricocheted ominously inside his

head as he replayed what she'd told him. Johnny inviting her to the family home on its private island...his last-minute call-back in the States... her decision to come without him. And, last but not least, he took in that teasing scrap of material she was wearing.

All of it could be explained away as either coincidence or misunderstanding. But the way she was biting into her lip and gazing up at him through that forest of eyelashes—that was calculated. It was the swift-thinking, self-serving, opportunistic response of a beautiful, unprincipled woman who knew her charms and was willing to turn them on for the right reward.

'No one. I'm obviously not working.'

Not on the clock, anyway.

He felt anger stir inside him. She might not have an Equity card, but she was one hell of an actress. Only she'd picked the wrong man to hustle.

'Not working. And *not* staying,' he said coolly.

Spinning round, he picked up her ridiculous pillarbox-red suitcase and tossed it onto the bed.

'Pack your stuff. You can spend the rest of the night here, but I want you out of my house in the morning. And out of my bed right now.'

She was staring at him open-mouthed, as if she couldn't believe what he was saying. He couldn't quite believe it either. He certainly hadn't been raised to turf guests out of their beds.

But Frankie Fox was not a guest.

He knew her type and she was all kinds of trouble wrapped up in a silk slip. Maybe another man—a more trusting, less experienced man, like Johnny—might be tempted to unwrap her. He knew better. It was the one, the *only* benefit of his short-lived, disastrous marriage to Harriet. Being able to look before leaping.

'You can't do this…' Her eyes were wide, and her mouth was trembling slightly. 'You can't just throw me out.'

'It's my home,' he said flatly. 'I can do what I like. And what I would like is to go to sleep. It's been a very long day, and tomorrow I've got a series of lectures to write up. Because, unlike you, I don't get paid to lounge around in my underwear. Nor am I running a B&B for my brother's cast-offs.'

Watching her hands clench, he knew she wanted to hurl her suitcase at his head.

'How dare you speak to me like that?' she hissed.

'Oh, I dare, Ms Fox.' He held her gaze. 'You see, I know exactly how this plays out. You came up here to play house with my sweet little brother, maybe "influence" him into something more serious. Only he bailed, so you're switching to Plan B. *Me.*'

'*What?*'

A slow wash of crimson flooded her cheeks as

the case slid from her fingers. But he refused to let his gaze drop to the tempting thrust of her breasts.

'Unfortunately, you're wasting your time. I'm on a break from women right now, and even if I wasn't, I would never be interested in some little chancer like you.'

She was looking at him as if he was something the tide had washed up on the beach.

'Let me get this right. You think *I* want to seduce *you*.' Hot colour flushed her cheeks like warpaint. 'As if!' She spat the words at him.

'Then you won't mind leaving my bed,' he snapped, more annoyed than he liked to admit by her emphatic response.

'Mind?' She scrambled to her feet. 'I'd rather sleep in the dog's basket than with you.'

'I wouldn't,' he said curtly, pulling his fleece over his head. 'He snores. And you can cut the theatrics. There's a whole other wing of bedrooms. But then I'm guessing you know that, from wandering around playing lady of the manor.'

The flush of colour darkened in her cheeks and with a rush of satisfaction he began unbuttoning his shirt.

'What are you doing?'

He could hear the sudden sharp snag of panic in her voice, but he didn't look over at her. 'I'm getting undressed.'

Unthinkingly, he shifted his gaze to the mirror over the fireplace and watched her snatch jeans and a jacket from the window seat. Her face and collarbone were still flushed pink and that glorious hair rippled over her bare shoulders like molten copper. She was exquisite.

His throat clenched. She was also about as far from his ideal woman as it was possible to get—and that was putting it mildly.

He swung round to face her, his eyes snagging on her bare legs before he had a chance to stop himself. 'Leave the keys.'

Breathing raggedly, she fumbled in the jacket pocket. As she pulled them out, they caught in the lining.

He swore softly. 'Here, let me—'

His fingers brushed against hers as he reached to help and he felt a sharp snap of static.

'Don't touch me.' Breathing out shakily, she jerked away from him.

He felt a stab of anger. He hadn't meant to touch her. Only now, as his eyes jumped from the fierce expression on her face to her soft parted lips, he realised he wanted more than one brief moment of contact. What he wanted was to push her back onto the bed and slide his hands over every inch of that satin-smooth skin...

'Nothing could be further from my mind,' he lied. 'Now, give me back the keys,' he said tersely.

Drawing a jagged breath, she tossed them at him and stalked across the room. As she reached the door she turned, tilting her chin to look at him with over-bright eyes, and he felt something twist inside his chest.

'You know, Johnny talks about you a lot. He thinks you're going to save the world...that you're a hero.' Raising her chin, she held his gaze. 'Some hero,' she said, smiling coldly.

And then, without giving him a chance to reply, she grabbed the handle of her suitcase and spun away into the darkness.

CHAPTER TWO

SHIFTING AGAINST HIS PILLOW, Arlo rolled over onto his side and opened his eyes reluctantly. There was a pale frame of light around the heavy curtains, so he knew it was morning. It just didn't feel like it.

He stretched his arms over his head. As he did so, his lurcher, Nero, sat up in his basket and looked wishfully at the four-poster bed.

'Stay,' Arlo warned as he sat up groggily.

Frowning, he rubbed a hand over his face. He'd wanted more than anything to sleep, and normally he didn't have any trouble—particularly during a storm. For some inexplicable reason he'd always found it oddly restful to lie in bed and listen to the weather rage like an impotent warlord against the house's thick walls.

Only last night had been different. He had spent most of the early hours of the morning twitching restlessly beneath the sheets in time to the drumming rain.

But then not much had been normal about last night.

His pulse stumbled. For starters, it had been a long time since he'd come home to find a woman in his bed.

He felt his throat close up. As for a woman wear-

ing next to nothing and brandishing a cricket bat…
That would be never.

Reaching over, he picked up the bat, weighing
it in his hand. He'd been hit by worse before. The
last time had been six months ago, on a field trip
to the Yamal Peninsula. He'd tried to break up a
fight in a bar in Murmansk, between a couple of
roughnecks celebrating payday, and had had his
nose broken with a pool cue for his trouble.

It wasn't the first time he'd had his nose broken,
but it had still hurt—a lot. As had the cracked ribs.
And yet if he had to choose, he'd almost rather be
hit any number of times with a pool cue than have
to remember Frankie Fox's parting words.

Some hero.

His jaw tightened.

Maybe he wasn't a hero to look at, but he had
the medals and the scars to prove his heroism—
scars that had come from bullets, not pool cues.
Yet those words and the expression of disdain on
Frankie Fox's face were what had kept him from
sleeping. Oh, and the faint scent of jasmine that
still clung to his pillow.

Irritably, he swung his legs over the side of the
bed and walked into the bathroom. Turning on
the tap, he ducked his head under the flow of cold
water.

Why was he letting some ridiculous, utterly ir-
relevant 'social media influencer' make him question himself?

Straightening up, he stared at his reflection. She hardly knew Johnny and she knew nothing about him. He gritted his teeth. But Frankie Fox had been right about one thing. His little brother idolised him.

They had always been close. It hadn't mattered that there was an eleven-year age gap or that they were very different people. Arlo was the difficult one. The brilliant high achiever with a double first from Cambridge and a doctorate in geology and earth science. Whereas Johnny...

His throat tightened. Everyone loved Johnny. It was impossible not to. He was beautiful, sweet-tempered, generous...

Too generous, he thought, stalking back into the bedroom. Yanking back the heavy curtains, he glared down at the turbulent grey sea outside. And some people—unscrupulous, self-serving people, like Frankie Fox—took advantage of that generosity.

He swore softly. Why was he even still thinking about that woman?

But he knew why.

He flexed his fingers, remembering the moment when their hands had touched. It had been more than skin on skin. It had felt oddly intimate. As if it had been their lips touching. There had been a charge of something electric.

They had both felt it...

Felt what? An imbalance of protons and electrons?

He scowled. It had probably been that silk thing she was wearing.

Great. Now he was back to thinking about her semi-naked.

Gritting his teeth, he reached down and stroked Nero's head, as if the action might erase the way her touch had jolted through his body.

Last night he'd been exhausted...disorientated.

Look at how it had taken tripping over her suitcase for him even to realise someone was in the house. If he'd been even halfway up to speed, he would have sensed that the moment he'd walked in the front door.

He ran a hand across his face, registering the slight resistance as his fingers grazed the scar on his cheek.

It wasn't just tiredness playing tricks with his mind. The truth was that since his marriage had imploded, he'd spent way too long on his own—and by choice.

He should never have got involved with Harriet in the first place.

Love, relationships, women...all of them came under the heading of 'Random, Imprecise, and Illogical'. In other words, everything he distrusted. So, aside from the occasional dalliance, he'd kept women at arm's length since.

And then, *boom*, out of nowhere there was Frankie Fox. Not just in his house but in his *bed*.

No wonder he'd got momentarily knocked off-balance. But whatever he'd imagined had happened in those few seconds had been just that. A figment of his imagination.

His lip curled.

Frankie, though, was real, and she was here in his home. And, despite her capitulation last night, he wasn't totally convinced that she would leave without a little persuasion.

Remembering the look she'd given him as she stalked out of the room, he felt his shoulders tighten.

Maybe if what had happened hadn't happened, he might have let her stay. There was obviously room and it wasn't as if he was in any danger. She might look like a living flame, but he'd put his hand in the fire once and that was enough for him to learn his lesson.

But he was here to work, and he didn't need any distractions. He didn't need to spend any more time with Frankie to know she would be a distraction with a capital D.

Constance could book her into a hotel for a couple of days and he'd offer to drive her to the station…

There was a low rumble of thunder and, glancing up at the darkening sky, he frowned.

He'd best get on with it.

This storm was going to be a big one.

Exactly six minutes later, he strode into the kitchen. He stared with satisfaction at the cream tiled walls and limed oak worktops.

After his father had retreated from the world much of the house had fallen into disrepair. The kitchen had been the first room he had renovated and, despite lacking the glamour and opulence of the drawing room, in many ways it was still his favourite.

'Good morning, Constance.' He glanced into the pan on the hotplate. 'Porridge—good! I'm absolutely starving.'

Constance swung round, her eyes widening. 'What are you doing here?'

Arlo felt a stab of irritation. First Frankie...now Constance. Why did everyone keep asking him that?

Turning towards the table, he frowned. 'Eating breakfast, I hope. Is that yesterday's paper?'

Constance ignored his question. 'I thought you were with Frankie.'

With Frankie!

Two small words. One big implication. Bigger than was necessary or welcome, he thought, as a tantalising image of what being *with Frankie* might encompass popped into his head.

Keeping his tone even, he shook his head and

replied. 'I haven't seen her.' He glanced up at the window. 'Storm's picked up.'

The wind sounded like a trapped animal whining and the rain was hitting the window with great wet smacks.

'She said you were taking her to the station...'

The cheeky little...

His jaw tightened. 'And I will. After breakfast.'

'But she left twenty minutes ago.'

It took two strides for him to reach the window that overlooked the causeway. The sky was the colour of a twelve-bore shotgun now, and it was raining so hard that it was impossible to see clearly. But he didn't need to see clearly to spot the blur of red inching along the raised cobbled road.

Gritting her teeth, Frankie gripped the handle of her suitcase more tightly and gave it a small, sharp tug.

Arlo Milburn had to be the rudest, most loathsome man she'd ever had the misfortune to meet, not to mention the most hard-hearted. What kind of host turned a guest out of their bed in the middle of the night? she asked herself angrily, for what had to be the hundredth time.

And as for his accusations—

She felt her heart scrabble inside her chest as her memories coalesced. Her shocked realisation that he was Johnny's brother... His cold-eyed disdain... That moment when the key had caught in her pocket and he'd tried to help her...

She replayed it silently inside her head, her fingers flexing involuntarily. His hand had been warm—warmer than she'd expected—the skin rough like sandpaper, and there had been a tiny but definite jolt of electricity.

Her mouth twisted. Arlo had been so tense with fury he could probably have single-handedly powered the entire coastline from here to John O'Groats.

She had no idea how he could be related to Johnny. But, then again, look at her and her super-high-achieving siblings. The twins had both been super-academic, sporty, and had won every prize going. Harry had been head-boy at school, and Amelie was practically a saint. With her blonde hair and sweet smile, she'd looked like an angel. Everyone had always been so surprised to find out Frankie was a Fox...

And now she was the only one left.

But this was not the time to go there. Right now, all that mattered was getting back to the mainland.

Screwing up her eyes against the rain, she stared down the causeway, trying not to give in to the panic rising in her chest. The wind was blowing so hard she could hardly keep hold of her suitcase and the rain felt more like hailstones. Worse, the waves were starting to slop over the cobblestones. *Was that supposed to happen?*

Her lower lip trembled. This whole trip had been a disaster. Basically, she'd spent five hours on a train to get shouted at and soaked to the bone. *Twice.* And to top it all, she'd overslept.

This was all Arlo's fault.

If he hadn't got her so wound up last night she wouldn't have slept through her alarm, and then she wouldn't have bumped into Constance, and Constance wouldn't have insisted that Arlo take her to the station...

Obviously she hadn't been about to hang around to be insulted again, so she'd pretended Arlo was waiting and sneaked out through the front door.

And it had seemed fine at first...

Her case slipped sideways again and, scowling, she gave the handle a savage jerk.

No, no, no, no... This could not be happening.

One of the wheels had popped out of its socket and was spinning away from her across the cobbles. She watched in dismay as it was swallowed up in a rush of water. Now she'd have to carry her case.

But as she turned to pick it up she felt something change amid the chaos.

Darkness.

As if the sky had turned black...

Looking up, she felt her heart slam into her ribcage, panic strangle her breath.

A huge, curling grey wave was rising out of the sea, towering over her.

For a moment, the air around her seemed to thicken and slow. And then the wave was falling, and the earth shifted on its axis, and then she was falling too, her feet slipping beneath her, her scream drowned out by an infinity of water...

From an immense, unfathomable distance, as though it had reached through the storm clouds, a hand grabbed her shoulder. Suddenly she was on her feet again.

Spluttering, gasping like a landed fish, she squinted up at her rescuer.

Arlo.

Water was sloshing around his feet, swirling and foaming across the cobbles. She caught a glimpse of dark, narrowed eyes, and then he scooped her into his arms as if she was made of feathers.

'Don't let go,' he shouted into her ear.

He turned back into the storm and the scream of the wind felt as if it was vibrating inside her bones like a shrieking banshee. Ahead, she could see nothing. The rain was like a curtain of water.

Her fingers tightened around Arlo's neck and she felt his shoulders brace. Then he bent his body into the gale, pushing forward, the only solid object in a swaying world. Dragging in a shallow breath, she turned her face into his chest, felt the heavy curve of his arm muffling the noise and the pounding rain.

Salt was stinging her eyes, and it hurt just to breathe, but she was not alone. Arlo was here. And she knew that, whatever happened, he would keep on going until he reached where he wanted to be.

A dark shape loomed out of the rain. It was a car, and as her chest hollowed out with relief, Arlo yanked open the passenger door, tossing her and her case inside.

He wrestled with the door and for a moment the roar of the storm filled the car. Then the door closed, and he was clambering into the driver's seat, and turning the key in the ignition.

'Hold tight,' he muttered. 'This could be tricky.'

They inched forward, the furiously swinging windscreen wipers having no impact on the rain thundering against the windscreen.

She clenched her hand around the armrest as a gust of wind sent the car staggering sideways, and then the car stopped and Arlo jumped out. Seconds later her door opened.

'Take my hand,' he yelled over the howl of the wind, and then he was pulling her forward.

They stumbled into the house. The huge front door crashed shut behind them and the high-pitched shriek of the storm faded like a whistling kettle taken off the heat.

Constance was standing in the hallway, her face pale with shock. Arlo's dark dog was beside her.

'Oh, my dear… Thank goodness you're all right. Come with me. There's a fire in the drawing room.'

Arlo glanced away, over his shoulder, his profile

cutting a broken line against the cream panelling. 'I'll get some towels.'

Frankie let the housekeeper lead her through the house. She was shivering so hard her chattering teeth sounded like an old-fashioned typewriter.

'Here, sit down. I'm going to make you some tea,' Constance said firmly.

Frankie sat down obediently on a large, faded velvet sofa and as the dog jumped up beside her lightly, she pressed her hand against his back. He felt warm and solid and, blinking back tears, she breathed out unsteadily.

Outside, in the screaming power of the storm, she had been robbed of the power of thought. It had been all she could do to cling to Arlo. Now, with the flames warming her body, her brain was coming back online.

Her fingers curled into the dog's fur as she pictured the scene on the causeway, her guilt blotting out any relief she might have felt at having been rescued. How could she have been so stupid? After everything that had happened. After all the promises she'd made to herself. To her family.

'You need to get changed.'

Her head jolted up at the sound of a deep, male voice. Arlo had walked back into the room, holding a pile of towels. Folded on top were a green-and-blue-striped rugby shirt and some sweatpants.

'Here.' He held out the pile. 'These are some of

Johnny's clothes. Your suitcase got drenched,' he said, by way of explanation.

He was staring down at her intently, and the flickering flames highlighted the hard angles of his face. He was soaked right though to his skin too, she thought guiltily. His shirt was sticking to his arms and body, and water was pooling in little puddles at his feet.

Picturing how he'd swept her into his arms like a knight without armour, she felt her heart beating too hard for her body. He'd saved her life. But, more importantly, he had risked his own.

She was about to apologise, to thank him for what he'd done, but before she could open her mouth, he said abruptly, 'They might be a little big, but they're clean and dry. I'll leave you to get out of those wet things.'

Glancing down at the dog, he frowned, moved as if to say something else, and then seemed to change his mind.

She watched him walk back out of the room, and then she stood up shakily. Her fingers were clumsy with cold, and it seemed to take for ever to peel off her jeans and sweatshirt, but finally she managed to get undressed and into Johnny's clothes. As she was rubbing her hair with a towel there was a knock at the door and Constance popped her head round.

'Oh, good, you've changed.' She was carrying a tray. 'I've brought you some tea and biscuits.' Leaning down, she picked up the pile of wet clothes. 'I'll just take these and run them through the washing machine.'

Frankie shook her head. 'Oh, no, please…that's really not necessary—'

'It is.'

Arlo was back. He had changed into faded chinos and a dark jumper that moulded around the contoured power of his arms and chest, and she had a sudden sharp memory of how it had felt to be pressed against his body.

'The salt will rot them if you don't wash it out.' He turned towards the housekeeper. 'Constance, could you give us a few moments? I need to have a couple of words with Ms Fox.'

As the door clicked shut, Frankie said quickly, 'Actually, I wanted to—'

'What the *hell* do you think you're playing at?'

Her chin jerked up as Arlo spun round, his eyes blazing. She stared at him, dry-mouthed, her heart pounding fiercely. Last night she'd thought he was angry, but now she saw that had been a warm-up to the main act.

'I'm not playing at anything—'

But he wasn't listening. 'So what was that little stunt of yours about?' He shook his head derisively. 'Let me ask you something. Do you know what that is out there?' He gestured to where the rain was slicing horizontally across the window. 'It's a storm *with a name*. Not all storms have names, but if they do that means there are winds of over fifty miles an hour.' His lip curled. 'There's also this thing called a *tide*. And twice a day there's a high tide. That means the sea is at its *highest*—'

'I know what a high tide is,' she snapped, her shock switching to anger at the condescension in his voice. 'I'm not a child.'

'Then why were you out there skipping down the causeway like a pre-schooler?' His cold gaze was fixed on her face, the pale line of his scar stark against the dark stubble. 'Did you think you could *influence* the weather? Make the sun shine? Stop the wind blowing?'

Stomach twisting, she struggled against a surge of humiliation and fury. 'I was doing what you told me to do. I was leaving.'

'What I told you to do—?' He rolled his eyes. 'I might have known this would be my fault.'

'I didn't say that'

'But you thought it.' His eyebrows collided in the middle of his forehead. 'Of course you did— because nothing is ever your fault, is it, sweet-heart?'

Her ribs tightened sharply at the memory of a different room on another rainy day. Not her fault officially, no. But the coroner's verdict hadn't changed the facts. She knew it had been her fault. All of it. That if she hadn't been so selfish, so in-sistent about getting her own way, then her family would still be alive...

Tears stung her eyes and the effort of not crying made her throat burn. Only she was not going to cry—not in front of him.

'Actually, Mr Milburn—'

The calm, bland expression on his face made her pulse shiver. 'Why so formal? I think we went past the "Mr Milburn" stage when you decided to get all warm and cosy in my bed.'

Her jaw dropped. She felt heat in her face, in her throat. Oh, but he was a horrible, horrible man.

Folding her arms, she took a deep breath. 'It's not my fault, *Mr Milburn*, that you're some boorish oaf who throws his guests out into the rain.'

He gave a bark of laughter. Only she knew he wasn't amused.

'Boorish oaf?'

The air crackled between them, and the snap of current mirrored the lightning forking through the sky outside.

His eyes narrowed and he stalked towards her.

Standing up, she held out a defensive hand. 'Stop—'

But he kept on coming as if she hadn't spoken, and she was struck again not just by his size, but by the sense of purpose beneath the layers of muscle and sinew and skin and by the intent in his eyes.

He stopped in front of her. 'Boorish oaf...' he repeated softly, his expression arctic. 'I just saved your life. Or have you forgotten how close you came to drowning?

Of course she hadn't.

For a few half-seconds she replayed the press of his hard chest against her cheek and how his arm had shielded her from the storm raging around them.

Her skin felt suddenly hot and tight. He had been so solid, so large. And, as ludicrous as it sounded now, he had seemed as implacable as the storm. As uncompromising and unyielding. She had wanted to burrow beneath his skin. To stay in the endless stretch of his arms with her head tucked under his chin...

Her heart bumped against her ribs. It was because he was implacable and uncompromising and unyielding that she'd been out on the causeway in the first place.

'You wouldn't have had to save my life if you hadn't been so horrible.'

His gaze raked her face like the lamp from a lighthouse.

'I think the word you're looking for is *truthful*,' he said coldly.

He ran his hand over his face, as if he wanted to wipe her out of his eyes, and her breath caught. She hadn't noticed it before but three of the fingers on his left hand looked too short, the tips oddly flattened.

She shivered inside. What kind of man was she dealing with?

'You know...' he spoke slowly, his dark gaze

locking with hers '… I thought you were just some clueless airhead who was hoping to get her claws into my soft-hearted brother.' His hard voice echoed around the room. 'But you are a *child*. A wilful, reckless child who wants everything her own way and when that doesn't happen throws a tantrum.'

The expression on his face made her skin sting. 'I—I'm not a child and I wasn't throwing a tantrum. I made a mistake—'

'And mistakes cost lives.' His voice was cold, each word more clipped than the last. As if he was biting them off and spitting them out. 'You're lucky it wasn't *your* life.'

Frankie blinked, tried to breathe, to swallow, but it was as if her heart was blocking her throat. She felt sick. It was true, and part of her had wanted, needed, to hear the truth for so long. Only it hurt so much more that she could have imagined.

'I'm sorry,' she whispered, and even though she was warm she was shivering again.

For months she'd been trying to hold it all together, but now she could feel her control starting to unravel—here in this room, with this stranger.

'You're right. I wasn't thinking about anyone but myself. I just wanted to go home. Only I can't—'

Not back to London. *Home,* home. But she could never do that again.

He was staring at her with those unyielding grey eyes and she took a shaky step backwards. *What was she thinking?* Had she really been about to tell Arlo the truth? Him, of all people? A man who clearly thought she was not worth saving.

And the trouble was, he was right.

Hot tears stung her eyes and the room blurred. 'I'm so sorry.' She gave a sob. 'I'm really, really sorry—'

Arlo watched in horror as Frankie stumbled across the room. He hadn't meant to upset her that much. It wasn't something he did: make women cry. Make *anyone* cry. Even with Harriet he'd been polite—courteous, even. It was only after they've broken up that he'd felt angry.

But that anger had been nothing in comparison to the head-pounding fury that had swept over him as he and Frankie had stumbled into the Hall.

How could she have done something so stupid, so reckless?

Worse than her recklessness, though, was the knowledge that he had driven her to it.

He'd wanted to scare her as she had scared him, so that she would think twice before she did something so foolhardy again.

His heart contracted as he thought back to the moment when he'd looked out of the kitchen window and seen her red suitcase bobbing jauntily along the causeway.

Those few minutes driving over the cobbles had been some of the longest in his life. Even now, the thought of her slipping beneath the swirling grey waves made his stomach lurch queasily.

'Frankie—'

She had reached the door and her fingers were tugging helplessly at the heavy brass handle. Before he knew what he was doing he had moved swiftly across the room. He thought she would tense as he pulled her against him, but she seemed barely to register him, and he realised that shock at what had so nearly happened out in the storm was finally kicking in. Or perhaps she had been in shock the whole time, he thought, as for the second time that day he scooped her into his arms.

'Shh… It's okay…it's okay.'

He carried her over to the sofa and sat down, curving his arm around her, holding her close as she sobbed into him.

Finally, he felt her body go slack and she let out a shuddering breath.

'Here.' He handed her a handkerchief. 'It's clean. And, more importantly, dry.'

She wiped her swollen eyes. 'Thank you.'

The wobble in her voice matched the shake in her hands as she held it out. He shook his head. 'No, you keep it.'

He watched as she pleated the fabric between her fingers, and then smoothed it flat, so that his initials were visible.

'I'm sorry,' she said shakily. 'For putting you in danger—'

'No, *I'm* sorry.' He frowned, wondering why it was so easy to say that now, when earlier herds of wild horses couldn't have dragged those words from his lips. 'If I hadn't kicked off at you last night you wouldn't have felt like you had to take that risk.'

Gazing down at her blotchy face, he felt a prickle of guilt. And he certainly shouldn't have kicked off at her just now—not when she was in such a state.

'I was tired, and annoyed with Johnny, and I took it out on you.'

'He did try and get in touch with you to tell you I was coming,' she said quickly.

Possibly... Johnny always had good intentions, and usually he found it easy to overlook his little brother's faults, but for some reason Frankie's defence of him got under his skin.

She looked up at him and the blue of her irises was so bewitchingly intense against her dark, tear-clotted lashes that he almost lost his train of thought.

He shrugged. 'I'm sure he did. Look, when the storm dies down a bit, I can take you to the station.'

She nodded. 'I'm sorry for making such a fuss. I'm just a bit tired. I've been working stupid hours...'

He understood tiredness. Sometimes out on the ice fatigue was like lead in his bones. But there was something more than tiredness in her voice... a note of despair, almost.

His jaw clenched. He understood that too, but Frankie was too young to feel that way.

He felt a stab of anger. Someone should be looking out for her.

Not him, though. Not after Harriet.

Her fingers smoothed out the handkerchief again and he felt her take a breath. Then she said quietly, 'I just want to say that it was really brave, what you did out there. Heroic, actually. So, thank you.'

She hesitated, and then he felt the flutter of her breath as she kissed him gently on the cheek.

The movement shifted her weight and she slipped sideways. Without thinking, he touched his hand against her hipbone to steady her. He heard the snap of her breath as she looked up, and when he met her soft blue gaze suddenly it was as if he'd run out of air. His head was spinning.

A minute went by, then another, and then she leaned forward and kissed him on the lips.

A voice in his head told him to stop her. That this was a mistake. That he didn't know this woman and what he did know he didn't like.

But then her fingers clutched at his shirt, drawing him closer, and he was lost.

It was like walking into a white-out.

There was nothing but Frankie. Nothing but the soft contours of her body and her mouth fusing with his.

His hands skimmed over her back, sliding up

through her hair, and he knew that this was not so much an exploration as an admission of his driving need to feel her, to touch every part of her.

He felt her soften in his arms and hunger jack-knifed through him as she leaned closer, so that her breasts were brushing against his chest. Blood pounded through his veins as he teased the upper bow of her mouth with his tongue, tracing the shape of her lips, and then he was guiding her onto his lap, pulling her restless hips against the hard press of his erection.

She moaned softly and, parting her lips, deepened the kiss.

He shuddered, heat flooding his limbs. Her mouth felt like hot silk and, groaning, he spread his hand over her back—

The sharp knock on the door echoed through the room like a gunshot and, peeling Frankie off his lap, he tipped her unceremoniously onto the sofa as he got to his feet.

What the hell was she playing at?

More to the point, what was *he* playing at?

Aside from the unspoken assumption that Frankie and Johnny were involved, this was a road he needed to travel less—not more.

His entire relationship with Harriet had been humbling and short—just under three months from that first kiss to the day she moved out—and he didn't need any more reminders of the idiocy of his behaviour.

Or maybe he did.

She stared up at him dazedly, her cheeks flushed, her lips swollen from his kisses.

Tearing his gaze away, he answered, 'Yes, what is it?'

'Douglas just called.' Constance's voice floated serenely through the door. 'They've issued an orange weather warning. I just thought you'd like to know.'

So the weather was causing road closures, interruption to power, and an increased risk to life and property. In other words, chaos.

Tell me something I don't know, he thought savagely.

Running his hand through his hair, he swore under his breath as his dazed brain finally registered the full implication of Constance's words.

An orange warning also meant being prepared to change plans. In this case, his plans to get Frankie off the island.

Jaw clenching, he glanced over at her.

'Looks like this storm is going to get worse before it gets better. Unfortunately for both of us, that means you're stuck here for the foreseeable future.'

Her eyes climbed up to his, a flush of colour engulfing the freckles on her face. 'Wow, you're a real Prince Charming.'

He held her gaze. 'What? A lovestruck fool chasing after a woman who can't keep her clothing on? You're in the wrong fairy tale, sweetheart.'

She gave him a look that could have stopped global warming in its tracks. 'You don't need to tell *me* that.'

His mouth twisted. 'Let me explain to you how this is going to work, Ms Fox,' he said. 'I don't want to see you. I don't want to hear you or talk to you. And above all I don't want to kiss you.'

'I don't want to kiss you either.'

She gave him an imperious smile that made him want to instantly eat his words.

'Good.' Stalking across the room, he yanked open the door. 'Stay out of my way. In fact, do us both a favour and stay in your room. Otherwise I might just be tempted to lock you in there until the storm passes.'

CHAPTER THREE

SLAMMING HER BEDROOM DOOR, Frankie stalked across the room, her heart pounding, her whole body trembling.

How dare he?

Her fingers clenched into fists.

Sending her to her room as if she was some child. And saying all that stuff about not wanting to see her or kiss her. As if she wanted to kiss *him*.

Her mouth twisted. Okay, to be fair, she had just kissed him—but it wasn't as if she'd planned it. And he was at least partly to blame…catching her off guard, his gentleness coming so fast after his anger.

Pulse twitching, she let her mind go back to the moment when she had lost her balance, and her brain conjured up his hand on her hip with such unflinching, high-definition clarity she could almost feel his precise firm grip…see the flare of heat in his eyes…taste her own urgent, unbidden desire to kiss him.

Not out of gratitude but out of a head-swimming hunger she'd neither questioned nor understood.

Remembering the noises she had made as his hands had moved over her body, she felt her face grow warm. It had lasted two, three minutes at most. It had been just a kiss...

Except something that had that kind of power—the power to make your heart stop beating—surely couldn't be *just* anything.

Not something, she corrected herself. *Someone.* Arlo Milburn.

He was like no one she'd ever kissed before. Older, more intense, beyond her comprehension and control. And yet she had wanted him like she had never wanted any man. And for those two, maybe three minutes she'd thought he wanted her in the same way.

Only then Constance had knocked on the door, and he had jerked back from her as if waking from a daydream.

Or a nightmare.

Her hands felt suddenly clammy. Clearly that was what he'd been thinking. Why else would he have pulled away? A hot blush of embarrassment spread over her skin as she remembered how he'd tipped her onto the sofa and quickly moved to put as much distance between them as possible.

Picturing his expression, she still wasn't sure whether he had been stunned or appalled at what had happened. Probably both.

Her brain froze. But then Arlo thought she was going out with his brother.

The heat in her cheeks made her feel as if her face was on fire. It was a testament to her current state of mind that she had completely forgotten about Johnny.

As Arlo's lips had touched hers, and he had pulled her against his big body, she had forgotten *everything*. It was as if her mind had been wiped clear.

But Arlo's hadn't.

Her stomach clenched.

Did he really believe she was with Johnny? That he was some kind of stand-in?

Oh, she felt awful. But why? Aside from one hug, nothing had happened with Johnny. And nothing had really happened with Arlo.

Just because there was no explanation for their kiss, that didn't make it significant. And perhaps there *was* an explanation. Both of them had just nearly died. Their emotions had been running high and all tangled up, so in some ways it had been almost inevitable that they would kiss.

She breathed out shakily. Hopefully at some point in the future she would be able to laugh about all of this, but in the meantime she was going to have to find a way to get through the next twenty-four hours.

Trying to still the jittery feeling in her legs that thought produced, she walked over to the window. Outside, the rain was still sheeting down, and both the sky and the violently cresting waves were the same dull gunmetal grey.

The weather forecasters had been right. It looked

as if this storm wasn't going anywhere any time soon, and that meant she was not going anywhere either. Only there was no way she was going to stay cooped up in this room until the wind blew itself out.

Arlo might be a man of many talents, but even he could only be in one place at once—and as there was both an east and a west wing, the chances of her bumping into him would be minuscule.

Maybe it was time to do a little exploring…

Obviously she had known the Hall was huge, but she was still stunned by the scale of it. There were just so many rooms, and each one seemed to be bigger and grander than the last. Everything was so perfect, she thought, as she gazed around an amazing book-lined library. And so perfectly English. From the plethora of patterns—chintz, checks, muted stripes—to the large, imposing portraits on the walls.

As she left the library and walked down the corridor her footsteps faltered in front of a half-open door. Behind it, a phone was ringing. It wasn't a mobile…it had an old-fashioned jangling sound.

Pinching her lip with her fingers, she hesitated, her shoulders tensing. Surely somebody would answer it…?

But the phone kept ringing, and before she had made a conscious decision to do so she was pushing open the door and walking into the room. It was some kind of office, judging by the two identical imposing wooden desks facing one another like duelling partners. Both were so cluttered with books and papers that it took her a moment to locate the phone.

She found it eventually, juddering beside a snow globe containing a polar bear. Heart pounding, she snatched it up.

'Hello—?'

But whoever it was had already rung off.

Typical. Rolling her eyes, she dropped the receiver back in its cradle. *Why did that always happen?*

Gazing around the room, she felt her breath rise with a rush into her throat. It was definitely an office, and it was equally obvious whose office it was. Her quick glance down at an in-tray overflowing with envelopes addressed to 'Dr Arlo Milburn' merely confirmed her suspicions.

She'd forgotten he was a Doctor of Geography. Or was it Geology?

Feeling as if she had wandered into the lair of some sleeping grizzly bear, she looked nervously round the room. Like the rest of the house, it felt both effortlessly grand but enviably comfortable.

What *was* surprising, though, was how untidy it was.

There were books everywhere. But not neatly stacked vertically on shelves, like in the library. Some were on shelves, but they were wedged in haphazardly. Elsewhere they rose in towering piles like stalagmites or huddled against pieces of furniture like snowdrifts.

Frowning, she glanced down at the paper-strewn desk. She'd expected someone like Arlo to be one of those 'tidy mind, tidy home' types, who thought a pile of letters demonstrated an inability to take command of a situation.

Remembering how he'd barked orders at her earlier, she curled her lip. He certainly liked telling people what to do, and it was hard to imagine him losing control.

Well, not that hard, she thought, her face growing hot and her lips tingling at the memory of how he'd pulled her against his body...

Quickly blanking her mind, she looked down at the chaos of paper, her gaze snagging on a notebook lying open. From this angle it was difficult to tell, but it looked like a sketch of a bird...a gull, maybe. Curious, she walked around the desk and sat down on the battered leather swivel chair.

It was just an outline—a few pencil marks, really—dated and annotated: *Pagodroma Nivea. Juvenile*. Then what looked like a map reference. Turning the page, she discovered more sketches and, her heart suddenly beating very hard, flicked through them.

They were good. Obviously drawn from life and by Arlo. Only she couldn't imagine him taking that moment of care and concentration to sketch anything. He was so vehement, so fierce. Surely his mere presence would make any self-respecting bird take flight…

This is lovely!

She touched a sketch of a seal pup. It was so lifelike she half expected to feel the fur beneath her fingertips.

Her eyes dropped to the notes beneath it. The handwriting was cramped and unfamiliar, and yet it *felt* familiar, comforting… Curling her feet up under her thighs, she started to read.

She recycled her plastics and tried not to use taxis when she could walk—but, truthfully, the environment had always been just another of those unfathomable, slightly intimidating big-concept words like 'the economy'.

But as she deciphered Arlo's notes she found herself not just curious but engaged. He wrote simply but eloquently, balancing the necessary use of scientific terms with obvious, unapologetic passion, so that she could almost see the frosted fields of ice with their exquisite lace of cracks and crystals. And Arlo, his grey eyes narrowed against the polar winds, his mouth—

His mouth… What about his mouth?

Pushing the notebook away, she picked up the snow globe instead, balancing it in her hands as she leaned back in the chair.

Her heart was still beating fast and out of time, as if she'd been caught in the act of doing something wrong. Which, in a way, she had, she thought, her brain tracking back to what had happened in the drawing room.

Only it hadn't felt wrong. Quite the opposite.

She tipped the snow globe upside down, watching the flakes swirl. Back in London, she had thought work, or rather too much work, was her problem, so she had come up here to relax and get some perspective.

Instead, she had nearly drowned, and then she had kissed Arlo, and now her head was even more overloaded.

Her chest tightened. It was stupid that he affected her this way. What she needed was to keep busy…

Her eyes flickered to the notebook, and she remembered what he'd said last night about writing up his lectures.

Could she work for him?

Her whole body stiffened in outrage at the question.

Absolutely not. Who in their right mind would want to work with Arlo?

He was rude and arrogant and high-handed. It would be like working for a dictator.

But, then again, it would be more a favour than actual employment…and only for a day or so. It would give her something else to think about other than his mouth… Plus, it would mean that he'd have to take her a little bit more seriously. Stop treating her like a cross between a disobedient child and some poor relation who had turned up uninvited for dinner.

And he *had* saved her life…

Pushing away from the desk, she let the chair swing slowly round in a slow circle until she was back where she started.

'Having fun?'

Her chin jerked up. Arlo was standing in the doorway, his mouth a thin line of contempt, Nero at his side.

She felt her stomach flip over.

He was scowling, and his dark hair looked as if he had run his hand through it too many times. A laptop dangled open from his hand.

'I was just—'

'Just what?' he snapped. His dark gaze swept around the room like a searchlight. 'You shouldn't be in here.'

'The phone was ringing.' She tried to smile. 'I came in here to answer it…'

She had been trying to do him a favour. Honestly, she wasn't sure why she'd bothered. But, then again, it probably *did* look as if she was snooping… Likely because she had been, she thought, a flush of heat creeping up to her ears.

'So who was it?'

'I don't know. They rang off just as I picked up.'

'How convenient,' he said coolly.

She glowered at him. 'What's that supposed to mean?'

'It means I don't think the phone was ringing. I think you wanted to have a nose around. Perhaps I can help? Were you looking for anything in particular?' The derision in his voice contorted his features. 'Something of value, maybe?'

Oh, that was low.

Her fingers curled around the snow globe. 'You know, it wouldn't hurt for you to be nice occasionally,' she said coldly.

He was staring at her as if she had suggested he might like to eat the contents of a wheelie bin.

'It wouldn't hurt for *you* to do what you're told.'

Her hands were gripping the snow globe so tightly she thought it might shatter. 'Who are you to tell me what to do?'

His dark grey eyes were like the slits in a castle wall. She half expected to see the tip of an arrow pointing out of each of them.

'Who am I? I'm your worst nightmare, Ms Fox.'

He stared at her, his hard, angular face dragging her gaze upwards.

'I'm a man who's immune to your charms. So I suggest you stop batting your eyelashes at me and go back to your room. And make sure you stay there. Otherwise, next time, I won't be feeling so generous.'

She stood up so suddenly that the chair spun

backwards. As it bounced off the shelves behind her, a pile of papers fluttered to the floor.

'You don't know the meaning of the word, *generous*,' she snarled. A beat of fury and frustration was pulsing over her skin. Her fists curling by her sides, she shook her head. 'You know, I can't believe I was actually going to offer to *help* you.'

Now he was staring at her as if she had grown horns or an extra head. '*You?* Help me?'

Trying to remember why she had thought it was a good idea, she glared at him. 'With writing up your lectures.'

He gave a bark of laughter. 'Why? So you can engineer a repeat performance of what happened downstairs?' Now he was shaking his head incredulously. 'I don't think so.'

She drew herself up to her full height. 'I didn't engineer anything.'

His flint-coloured eyes were cold. 'You kissed a perfect stranger. I would have thought that required a little forethought—unless, of course, you do that with every man you meet.'

Her hands were trembling, and she was nearly breathless with anger. No, actually, she didn't. As a matter of fact, she'd only kissed a handful of men—and none with the unthinking urgency with which she had kissed him.

Lifting her chin, she glared at him. 'I'm sorry to disappoint you, Mr Milburn, but you're a long way from my idea of perfect.'

The skin on his face stretched taut, like a drum, and she felt the air grow charged, as if the storm had moved inside.

'As you are mine. I mean, aside from the quite obvious fact that you lack the discipline and diligence I would expect from anyone who works for me, I'm not sure you have the specialist knowledge I need. I mean, what exactly do you know about ice anyway?'

The curl of his lip made her want to throw the snow globe at his head.

'Other than crushing it for frozen margaritas at a "fun girls' night just for you"?'

His words sounded familiar.

Her jaw started to tremble. That was because they were *her* words—from the blog she had posted last summer. She breathed out shakily. The idea of Arlo reading her blog made the anger leak out of her like air from a burst balloon.

Her heart thudded heavily in her chest. She felt stupid and shallow and superfluous. But then that was what she was. It was just that in the heat of their argument she had momentarily forgotten.

Arlo saw her stiffen and swore under his breath.

Finding her in his office, curled up in his chair, had caught him off balance more than he'd ever be willing to admit.

She had been pinching her lip—a habit she seemed to have when she was thinking—and, watching her press her fingers into that cushion of flesh, he had felt a rush of too-predictable heat tighten his muscles.

It had been a shock to discover than he could still be so weak, so hungry for what was so obviously wrong for him, and he'd felt angry and frustrated with himself. Angry, too, with her, for exposing this weakness in him.

Maybe he had been a little brutal, but it wasn't as if he was going to take her up on her offer. The idea was ludicrous.

Or was it?

Gazing over at Frankie, he pondered the question.

Perhaps, in a way, her working for him wasn't such a bad idea, given the facts—which were that he had no idea how long the storm would take to blow itself out, and that Frankie would be here in the house with him until it did. Giving her a job would not just keep her out of mischief, it would put their relationship on a more formal footing and provide clear boundaries.

'What did you mean by help?' he asked slowly.

She stared at him mutely, then said, 'If that's your version of an apology you might want to do a little work on it.'

His eyes locked with hers. *Apologise for what?* She was in his office, uninvited—

With effort, he reined in his temper. Right now,

there was enough turmoil outside—he didn't need to add to it.

Unlocking his jaw, he took a breath. 'I'm sorry for what I said.'

He waited as she shifted from one foot to the other, her expression guarded.

'I'm sorry too,' she said finally. 'I shouldn't have come into your office without asking. I wouldn't have done, but your phone was ringing, and I thought it might be important.'

Her apology surprised him almost as much as her offer of help, and for a moment he wondered if he'd misjudged her. But it wasn't easy to get his head around the idea that he might have been wrong—partly because he still thought she was inherently self-serving, and partly because it reminded him that he'd been so wrong about Harriet and was supposed to have learned and moved on from the experience.

Pushing that thought away, he nodded. 'If the offer is still there, I'd like to take you up on it. You'd be doing me a favour,' he added, when she didn't reply.

'I *would* have been, yes.'

'You still could,' he said carefully.

Her eyes widened. 'So you can laugh at me again?'

'I wouldn't laugh—'

Glancing away, she shook her head again. 'I'd be no use to you. Like you said, I'm only interested in the kind of ice that comes in a glass. I don't know the first thing about vertical migration or hydrofracture.'

Vertical migration… Hydrofracture…

Arlo frowned. How the hell did she know about those? Unless—

'You read my notebook.'

She gazed back at him, her chin jutting forward.

'So what if I did? I'm not going to share it with my followers, if that's what you're worried about.'

'No, I mean you can read my writing.'

She looked at him, confusion warring with curiosity, then shrugged. 'My father was a doctor.'

Her tone told him that she was not entirely sure why she was telling him that fact.

'Everyone thought his writing was illegible, but I grew up with it so…'

'Is that why you offered to help me?'

She shrugged again. 'I don't know. It felt like the least I could do. I mean, you did save my life.' She glanced away. 'And I'm not working at the moment.'

What did that mean? He knew almost nothing about the mechanics of social media, but what little he did know suggested that it was a twenty-four-seven, three-hundred-and-sixty-five-days-a-year kind of gig.

Not that it was any of his business… And yet he found himself wondering what it was she wasn't telling him.

Watching her pinch her lip again, he tamped down the urge to reach over and pull her hand away and then cover her mouth with his.

His jaw clenched, and suddenly he needed her to agree. 'Look, Frankie, I know we got off on the wrong foot, but this storm is going to be kicking around for a couple of days and that means we're going to be—'

'Stuck with each other?' Her eyes met his. 'Not if I stay in my room, like you told me to.'

'I shouldn't have said that either. I was just—'

Just scared. Scared of what would happen if they came within touching distance of one another. Scared that he would give in to that same desperate, urgent desire that had swept him away as effortlessly as one of those towering grey waves outside.

'Just being a boorish oaf.'

There was a pause.

'Is it just transcribing?' she asked.

He felt a jolt of surprise. 'You've done this before?'

Her eyes slid away from his, and he had that same feeling as before—as if she was holding back.

'My older brother and sister both did dissertations. They paid me to type them up.'

He nodded. 'Okay, well, there's a bit of an overlap between my notes on the web and the ones I had to write by hand, but I can talk you through that. It would help, too, if you could answer the phone. Take messages if I'm on the other line.'

There was a pause. He could almost see her working through the pros and cons.

She sighed. 'Okay. I'll do it. But just so we're clear, I'm working *with* you, not for you.' Lifting her chin, she let her hair fell back from her face so that he could see the curve of her jawline. 'I'm not having you bark orders at me—'

He held up his hands in appeasement.

'There will be no barking. Although I can't speak for Nero.'

A reluctant smile pulled at the corners of her mouth, softening her face, and suddenly it was difficult to find enough breath to fill his lungs. If she kept smiling like that then maybe the dog kennel might be the safest place for him.

'Good. That's sorted. Take a seat.' He gestured towards the other desk. 'And we can get started.'

The morning passed with almost hallucinatory speed. One moment Frankie was walking across the room to the other desk, and the next Arlo was pushing back his chair and telling her it was lunchtime.

Gazing round the beautiful dining room, with its cream panelling, carved wood fireplace and oil paintings, she felt her heartbeat accelerate. Mostly, if she was at home, lunch would be a sandwich eaten at her desk—and then only if she could be bothered to make one. More often than not it was just a bowl of cereal.

This, though, was a sit-down three-course meal, with cutlery and napkins and side plates...

'Everything okay?'

Arlo was staring at her, his face arranged in one of those unreadable expressions.

'Everything's fine.' She glanced down at her starter: a tartlet of smoked roe, tomato, and marjoram.

'It's just that when you said, "Let's grab some lunch", I was expecting something a little more basic.'

'What did you think? That we'd be gnawing on reindeer bones—'

She smiled faintly. 'Something like that.'

Reaching for his knife and fork, he shrugged. 'I've spent the last few months eating polar pâté three times a day with a spork. When I get home, I like to eat real food at a table.' His eyes rested on her face steadily. 'It's one of my rules.'

Her brain picked over his words. *One of his rules.* What were the others?

Picking up her glass, she took a sip of water. Earlier, she'd asked herself who would want to work with him. The answer, surprisingly, was pretty much anyone and everyone, judging by the number of calls she'd answered in the hour before lunch. The phone had rung almost non-stop.

The Smithsonian Institution, the Royal Geographical Society, and Stanford University had all asked him to speak, and after just sixty minutes in his company it was not hard to see why. Listening to him talk, it had become clear to her that Arlo knew his stuff. More importantly—and, she was guessing, more unusually in a scientist—he was both concise and eloquent.

She liked the sound of his voice, the strength of it, and the measured, precise way he chose his words. And he spoke Russian fluently.

Of course, she *didn't* speak Russian, so she had no idea what he'd been talking about when he'd spoken it on the phone, but it had sounded almost like poetry.

He looked like a poet too. Or maybe a cross between a poet and pirate, with his scowl and his messy hair and that complicated mouth.

Although it hadn't felt that complicated when they were kissing...

As if he'd heard her thoughts, Arlo looked over at her, his grey eyes boring into hers. She put down her glass and over the sudden, rapid beat of her heart said quickly, 'I can imagine.'

He shifted back in his chair, his dark sweater stretching endlessly across his shoulders. 'Stop fidgeting and eat something,' he said.

'I'm not fidgeting.'

'Just eat,' he ordered. 'I don't want you passing out on me.'

'I've never passed out in my life,' she protested.

He stared back at her impassively, a comma of dark hair falling across his forehead to match the white scar on his cheek.

'So?' Leaning forward, he speared a piece of tomato on his plate. 'You nearly drowned this morning. I don't suppose that's a regular occurrence, *ergo* there's a first time for everything. Now, eat.'

She stared at him, exasperation pulsing down her spine. 'Have you always been this bossy?'

He hesitated, as though seriously considering her question. Then, 'I would say so, yes.'

Picking up her cutlery, she rolled her eyes. 'I bet you were a prefect at school.'

There was a pause and, watching his lips almost curve, she felt the air leave her body.

'Actually, no.'

'Really? Finally, we have something in common,' she said lightly.

Their eyes locked, hers teasing, his serious, and then he nodded. 'It would appear so.'

Suddenly she felt as if the room had shrunk. Or maybe the table had. Either way, it felt as if they were sitting way too close.

There was another small pause, and then he smiled. 'Now, eat.'

As he turned his attention back to his plate her fingers tightened around the knife and fork. Some people's smiles—Johnny's, for instance—were just a part of them. But Arlo's was miraculous, transformative, softening the blunt, uncompromising arrangement of his features into something far less daunting.

She silently fought against an urge to reach out and trace the swooping curve of his mouth. A mouth that held and delivered an urgency of promise...

As if sensing her gaze, Arlo looked up and, not wanting him to notice her flushed cheeks, she bent her head over her plate.

For a moment they ate in silence.

'Good?' He raised one dark eyebrow.

She nodded. It was melt-in-the-mouth delicious, the pastry literally crumbling under her fork.

In fact, it was all delicious. The main course of silky pappardelle with beef shin ragu was followed by a tart Amalfi lemon sorbet and then coffee.

Leaning back in his seat, Arlo gave her a levelling glance, his dark eyes roaming over her face. 'You were pale before. You have colour in your cheeks now.'

Her heart started to beat very fast.

He had the most intense gaze of any man she'd ever met. It felt as if it was pushing through her skin...as if he was inside her.

Inside her.

Her pulse twitched as the words repeated inside her head and blood surged through her, so that for a moment she forgot what they were talking about, forgot where she was, *who* she was.

Looking away, she cleared her throat. 'It's been a long day and a lot has happened.'

He nodded but didn't reply. A few seconds ticked by, and then he said abruptly, 'Yes, about that...'

Her stomach dropped as if he'd just pushed her out of a plane. She stared at him, the skin on her face suddenly hot and tight. 'What about it?'

'We haven't really discussed what happened earlier.'

No, they hadn't—thankfully.

She glanced out of the window. Outside, the wind was rearranging the trees that edged the garden.

It was unsettling enough having the whole episode playing on repeat inside her head. She didn't need or want to replay it in front of this man with his dark, intent gaze.

Unfortunately avoiding it might not be an option.

Picturing his expression as he had carried her back to the car out on the causeway, the relentlessness in his eyes as he'd pushed back against the wind, she felt a tremor ripple through her.

Arlo Milburn was definitely the tackle-things-head-on type.

Turning her eyes to his, she shrugged. 'There's nothing to discuss. It was—'

'A mistake?' he asked.

'Yes.' She nodded vigorously—perhaps too vigorously, she thought a moment later, watching his face harden. 'Or maybe not a mistake...more a misunderstanding.'

'You think?' He shifted back his seat, his dark brows rising up his forehead. 'It seems fairly unambiguous to me. You kissed me and I kissed you back.'

'I suppose that's one way of looking at it,' she said slowly.

'What are the other ways?'

Goosebumps skittered down her spine as she struggled to put together a coherent sentence, or at least one she could say out loud. In other words, nothing about feeling that he hadn't only rescued her out on the causeway but *claimed* her...

'I think of it as more of a cosmic chain reaction,' she managed. 'You know...when things collide... like stars, planetary forces...'

'And lips?' Her insides tightened as he held her gaze.

'I suppose you believe Elvis is alive too?' He shook his head dismissively. 'I'm only interested in facts, not half-baked theories.'

'Not everything can be explained by facts,' she retorted, stung by his manner. 'Some things just happen.'

Except they didn't, did they? Everything that happened, however 'accidental' it seemed, was the consequence of a collection of facts, decisions made, paths taken, feelings overruled...

The details of the dining room were blurring around her in the silence. She shivered. And it didn't matter if some of those facts stayed hidden, they were still true. They would always be true.

'Like what?' he asked.

He was staring at her in silence and, momentarily trapped in his gaze, she held her breath. Should she tell him the truth? That he was right. That nothing was random. That there was always a reason, always something or someone responsible—

Pushing back her chair, she stood up. 'Look, Mr Milburn, interesting as this conversation is, I thought we had work to do.'

'It's Arlo—and we do,' he said calmly. 'That's why I wanted to talk to you about what happened in the drawing room. To reassure you. You see, I don't believe in mixing business with pleasure. It never ends well.'

Frankie blinked. She took a deep breath. Just for a moment she had almost liked him. She'd even thought he liked her. And all because of one stupid, unthinking kiss.

But that kiss hadn't changed anything. It certainly hadn't changed him. He was still the same rude, arrogant man who had turfed her out of bed.

'That's sweet of you.' Angling her chin up, she smiled thinly. 'But you don't need to worry on my account. I've practically forgotten it ever happened.'

CHAPTER FOUR

LEANING BACK IN HIS CHAIR, Arlo extended his arm over his back, grimacing as he stretched out his neck. A pulse of frustration beat down his spine. They were back in his office, and as a gust of wind shook the house he stared out of the window to where the waves were flinging up foam.

Usually, he found it easy to work. But not today, he thought, glancing down at the cursor blinking reproachfully at the top of the blank page on his computer screen. Today he'd struggled to find one word that could hold his attention long enough for him to forget that Frankie was in the room.

His eyes narrowed on the halo of auburn curls that was just visible over the piles of books on the other desk. It was unconscionable to let a woman—*this* woman—distract him from work. Work that was, after all, the only reason she was here in his office. Although now he was finding it hard to remember why he had ever thought that was a good idea…

Shifting back in his seat, so that he could no longer see the top of her head, he watched his screen go black.

He hadn't been lying when he'd told Frankie that he was on a break from women. A long break, as it happened—maybe too long. But it was through choice rather than lack of opportunity. He'd deliberately let the expeditions, the lecturing, the research, take precedence over his love life.

It was easier that way...less painful.

Love was for fools. Or maybe it made people into fools. Either way, he'd decided a long time ago that it was too unpredictable to make it the basis of any relationship other than a familial one.

Of course, familial love was no less painful. But at least it played by the rules. It was logical. Naturally, a mother might love and support her child, a father his son, a boy his brother. It was hardwired into their DNA.

Love between a couple was different: dangerous. It didn't matter if it was based on duty or desire, it lacked any real scientific foundation. Lust, on the other hand, was the engine in the juggernaut of life. It was a simple compulsive force—like gravity. Potent. Persuasive. Undeniable.

Thinking back to the uppity put-down Frankie had thrown at him after lunch, he felt anger coil up inside him like a snake. He had felt like running after her and shaking her. Or, better still, kissing her. Kissing her until she melted into him as she had done that morning.

'I've practically forgotten it ever happened.'

Who was she trying to kid?

Unclenching his jaw, he shifted forward.

'Could you please stop fidgeting?' Frankie's

voice floated up from behind the desk. 'Some of us are trying to work.'

A rush of heat tightened his muscles. 'Are you talking to me?'

She sighed audibly. 'Well, I'm not talking to Nero.'

As the dog lifted its head from the floor Arlo hesitated and then, pushing back his chair, stood up and walked across the room.

'It wouldn't matter if you were. You see, unlike you, he prefers it when people bark.'

'And I prefer it when people are straight with me.' Her eyes narrowed. 'I thought you wanted my help.'

'I do.'

'Then what's with all the huffing and puffing?'

'I wasn't aware I was huffing and puffing,' he lied. 'It's just transitioning back to working behind a desk...it's hard after so many weeks out on the ice.'

His jaw tightened. She was looking at him as if she thought that level of sensitivity was beyond him. But he could be sensitive when required. In fact, he could be anything she wanted—

His body tensed as he remembered her breathless little gasp when he'd pulled her hips against his body.

'I haven't changed my mind. You're doing a good job.' Clearing his throat, he gestured towards the shelves behind her desk. 'Actually, I need to check something in one of those files. The blue one,' he said, pointing at one at random.

She got to her feet, her eyes travelling over the haphazardly stacked shelves. 'You have really great organisational skills.'

He tapped his head. 'It's all up here. I know where everything is. No, I can get it myself. No, let me—'

Reaching up, he made a grab for the file, but she was already tugging at it.

'Ouch!'

Books and files were tumbling from the shelf, and he swore as one hit him squarely on the bridge of his nose.

'Why don't you ever do what you're told?' The pain was making his eyes water. 'I said I'd get it.'

Frankie glared up at him. 'You know, I'm getting really tired of how everything is always my fault with you,' she snapped.

'Not as tired as I am of nothing ever being your fault,' he snapped back.

'I didn't say that...' Pressing her hand against her head, she winced.

'Are you hurt?'

She shook her head, but as she lifted her hand, he felt his pulse jump into his throat.

'You're bleeding—'

'It's nothing.'

'It's not nothing.' He led her to the sofa. 'Sit.'

She pushed against his hand. 'I'm not a dog.'

Damn, she was stubborn. She was also bleeding. He took a breath. 'Please could you sit down?'

With relief, he watched her drop down onto the cushions. Angling the lamp to see better, he grabbed her chin between his thumb and forefinger.

'Look up. *Please*,' he added as she stiffened against his hand.

He parted her hair. 'Okay, it's a small cut. It's not bleeding much, but you'll probably have a bit of a bump.'

She sighed. 'I don't need a nurse.'

'Lucky I'm a doctor, then,' he said.

Her eyes narrowed. 'Of rocks. And ice. Not people. Now, if you've finished?'

'I haven't.' He fished out a handkerchief from his pocket. 'Press this here. I'm just going to get the first aid box. And don't even think about moving.'

Leaning back against the sofa cushions, Frankie closed her eyes and breathed out shakily. It was Arlo's fault, she thought angrily. If he had organised his shelves like any normal person this wouldn't have happened.

Her head was throbbing and there was a metallic taste in her mouth, and she felt a nauseous rush of *déjà vu*. Clutching the arm of the sofa, she opened her eyes and steadied herself.

That had been her first memory after the accident that had killed her entire family. Eyes closed, her head hurting inexplicably. She hadn't understood at first. She had felt as if she was dreaming, only then she'd opened her eyes and realised the nightmare was real.

'Sorry I took so long. How are you feeling?'

Arlo was back. She gazed up at him, frowning. 'Fine. It's really not that bad.'

'I'll just spray some antiseptic on—'

He was being so nice, and his touch was gentle in a way that made her throat ache more than her head.

'What happened here?' he asked.

His fingers had stilled against her head, and she knew that he had found the thin line of puckered skin.

According to the French media it was a miracle she had survived the crash. Afterwards, when she'd seen photographs of the plane, it had been hard to believe she had not just survived but walked away with just one tiny reminder of what had happened that night in France.

Only one visible reminder, anyway.

Balling the handkerchief in her hand, she shrugged. 'I was in an accident. A couple of years ago.'

She couldn't see his expression, so she didn't know what he was thinking, but she did know she wanted to stay in control of this particular conversation.

'I banged my head. It left me with a healthy respect for safety belts and this scar.'

That was true. Not the whole truth and nothing but the truth. But she had never told anyone that except at the inquest, and that had been an experience that had taught her not to expect justice even from those charged with dispensing it.

'So we have something else in common,' she said lightly. Looking up into his face, she widened her eyes. 'Oh, but you're hurt too.'

'What? This?' Reaching up, he touched the dark bruise at the bridge of his nose. 'It's nothing.' He smiled. 'It's hardly going to mar my good looks, is it?'

'You *are* good-looking.'

His forehead creased into a frown. 'Maybe I need to take a closer look at that bump...'

She bit into her lip and he held her gaze.

'It's okay. Johnny's my brother. I know what beauty looks like.'

Conventional beauty, she thought. Or perhaps it would be better named conformist beauty.

Johnny was Michelangelo's *David*. All perfect lines and symmetry. And yet for some reason she couldn't quite picture his face anymore.

Her heart smacked against her ribs.

There was nothing symmetrical about Arlo. He was a rough draft, formed by a more urgent hand. An Easter Island profile chipped in bone, not rock.

A man who corrected the course of everything in his path.

Glancing up, she felt a jolt of electricity crackle up her spine as their eyes met.

'Beauty is God's handwriting. It's not legible to everyone.'

There was a long pause, and then his eyes fixed on her face. 'But it is legible to you?'

Her heart thudded hard. She felt something stir inside her, as if there was a storm building there…

'Doctor's daughter,' she said, breaking the taut silence. 'So, Arlo, tell me—what made you want to go to Antarctica?'

For a few half-seconds, Arlo didn't reply. Not because he didn't know the answer. He had been trying to work out why she had changed the subject, only the sound of his name on her lips seemed to have momentarily stopped his brain working.

Just seconds earlier he'd been trying to remember why he'd thought it a good idea to give her a job.

Something about putting her off-limits—that was it. An imbalance of power.

Now that decision felt premature on so many levels…not least because he felt uniquely and perilously at a disadvantage.

Hoping his silence suggested that he was taking her question seriously, rather than taking leave of his senses, he dragged his gaze away from her soft pink mouth.

'When I was twelve years old, I read *The South Pole* by Roald Amundsen. I found it gripping. The menace and the mercy of nature. There's a copy in the library if you want to read it. Second shelf on the level as you walk in.' His eyes met hers. 'Don't worry. The books are a lot better behaved downstairs.'

She smiled then, and suddenly it was his turn to change the subject.

'So how are you finding the work? Not too dry, I hope?'

'Not at all.' She hesitated, then, 'Actually, your notes are surprisingly interesting.'

'Thank you. I think,' he said, the corners of his mouth pulling up very slightly.

'It's just that there's a lot of numbers. You know...percentages of this and metric tons of that.'

He frowned. 'In other words, facts.'

'Exactly.' She stared at him impatiently, as if he was missing something glaringly obvious. 'I know you love facts, but most people find them really intimidating, so you have to make them interesting and understandable. And you have. I mean, if someone like me can understand them you must have done.'

'What do you mean, "someone like me"?'

She bit her lip. 'You know... Someone who lacks "discipline and diligence".'

There was a small, stiff silence as he replayed her words—his words, in fact—inside his head. 'Look, I wasn't thinking straight this morning. I was still angry and scared—'

Her chin jerked up. 'Scared?' She screwed up her face as if she didn't believe him. 'Of what?'

He hadn't meant to admit his fear out loud, and now he felt his body tense as he remembered that grey wall of water rising up around her. Remembered, too, the promise he had made to himself all those years ago. Never to let fear overrule facts. Never to let the preventable become the inevitable.

'Scared that you'd be hurt.' *Or worse.*

Frankie was staring at him in silence. 'I thought you hated me...'

They were so close he could see each and every freckle on her face. He wondered how long it would take to count them. And where exactly they stopped on her body.

He cleared his throat. 'I don't hate you.'

He heard her swallow. 'I don't hate you either.'

His breath stalled as her eyes rose to his face. Gazing down, he could see the pulse at the base of her throat beating in time with the blood pounding through his veins.

He was powerless to look away.

Time seemed to soften and then stop.

Their legs were touching at the knee...her hand was just inches from his. Never in his life had he wanted to kiss a woman so badly...

But before he could wrap his hand around her neck and bring her mouth to his, the grandfather clock at the end of the room chimed the hour.

She blinked, as if waking from a dream. 'It that the time? Constance said supper was at a quarter past.'

As she got to her feet Arlo frowned up at her. 'You know what? I've just remembered I need to call a couple of people back. But you don't need to wait for me—in fact, you shouldn't. Tell Constance I'll sort myself out in a bit.' Standing up, he walked over to his desk. 'And take Nero with you, will you? Otherwise, he'll just bug me to feed him.'

He made his calls and then, wanting to prove to himself that he could, he sat down and waded through his notes.

Finally, Nero came padding back upstairs. It was ten o'clock. 'Okay, then.' Pulling the dog's silky ears, he followed him downstairs, but instead of heading to the kitchen, Nero trotted down the corridor.

He followed him into the library. It was dark, but the fire was still glowing, and opposite the fire Frankie was asleep on the sofa, a disorder of curls framing her face, the Amundsen book open beside her.

His shoulders tensed.

Should he move her? Probably not. She might freak out—and anyway that would mean taking her up to her bedroom.

He felt his body grow taut. He'd been shot, punched, and he'd suffered frostbite, but the idea of sliding Frankie's body beneath the sheets and then having to walk away was a new, excruciating pain.

Leaning forward, he gently added a couple of logs to the fire and then, tugging a throw off the back of the sofa, he draped it over her body.

His jaw tightened. Now what? Sleeping on one of the other sofas seemed like a bad idea, but he didn't want to leave her alone.

He glanced down at Nero. And he didn't have to. 'Up,' he said quietly, watching the dog jump up onto the sofa and curl into a ball. 'Now, stay.'

Body twitching, Arlo turned and walked swiftly out of the library, and away from a sudden, inexplicable desire to trade places with his dog.

When Frankie woke the sky was light.

She had been dreaming of Antarctica, sleep-walking across blue-shadowed frozen oceans, and for a few half-seconds the light pressing against her eyelids felt like the solid white sun shimmering above that endless polar landscape.

Except it was far too warm to be Antarctica.

Yawning, she opened her eyes and sat up.

At the end of the sofa Nero lifted his head, his tail thumping against the armrest. Her body tensed. Nero meant Arlo.

Heart pounding, she glanced over her shoulder. But the library was empty. She was alone.

She felt a flush heat her face. She hadn't been alone last night—at least not in her dreams. Arlo had been with her, always just out of reach and hazy, as if he was walking through mist.

Her stomach did a clumsy little flip. It sounded weird, putting it like that, but dreams told you what you already knew. Her dream was simply proving that she found Arlo baffling.

Satisfied with that explanation, she patted the dog's tousled head, her eyes following his gaze to the windows.

Surprise chased away her unease.

The trees in the garden were no longer bending over like supplicants and the sky was a dirty white instead of battleship grey.

Glancing at the clock above the fireplace, she frowned. It was too early for breakfast.

'Come on, then,' she said softly. 'Let's go and get some fresh air.'

Outside on the slopes a fine mist was making it hard to see the sea, but beneath her feet the short salt-soaked grass was speckled with tiny vivid pink-and-blue flowers.

Up ahead, Nero was bounding around in circles, clearly ecstatic at being able to have a proper run, and he was barking, yelping in excitement at something—

Not something. Someone. Arlo.

She felt a buzz go through her body.

He was walking out of the mist towards her, just as he had in her dream, his dark hair falling in front of his eyes, his long legs making short work of the springy turf.

She stared up at him, her blood turning to air, her vision shuddering in and out of focus. He was bare-chested, with a black sweater tied around his waist and, incongruously, a dark sheep, complete with curling horns, draped over his shoulders.

Her mouth felt as if it had been sandpapered.

He looked like someone from another age and he seemed completely at ease—as if he often stripped off to the waist and carried livestock around. Her gaze dropped to his chest…to the acreage of pale muscle.

When he had picked her up on the causeway, and then again when she had kissed him, she'd had a sense not just of physical strength but of a potent, untapped power.

Now she knew why.

He was not just 'ripped', there was a kind of organic solidity to his physique—almost as if his upper body was made of stone. And yet there was nothing clumsy about the way he moved. On the contrary, he had the same easy, loping gait as the dark dog that was now trotting beside him.

At that moment Arlo looked up, and her stomach clenched as if it was being squeezed by a giant hand. She watched him come closer, nervously trying out various half-finished sentences in her head. And then he was stopping in front of her, and suddenly it was a struggle to fill her lungs, much less think in sentences. Above them, the sky seemed to shrink back on itself.

'Good morning.'

He gave her a slight almost-smile and, even though he was the one who was half naked, she felt herself blushing.

'Are you looking for me or just out for a walk?'

His dark grey eyes rested on her flushed face and, trying to control the hammering of her heart, she said quickly, 'A walk.'

Dragging her gaze away from the thin line of dark hair that disappeared into the waistband of his jeans, she looked up at the sheep. 'What happened to it?'

His forehead corrugated into a frown. 'It's difficult to say. Either she hunkered down in the wrong place or she got blown over by the wind. She doesn't seem hurt, but she didn't want to move. She's probably just winded.'

'Where did you find her?'

'Just over there.'

She followed his gaze. The mist had cleared, and she felt a kick of horror. Maybe the slope was less steep when you were standing on it, but from this angle the gradient looked almost vertical.

'You went down there?' Her horror morphed into outrage. 'Imagine if *I'd* done that.'

His eyes met hers. 'Why would you? You don't have anything to prove.'

And he did? She stared at him in confusion. He was a decorated soldier, an expert in his field, *and* a polar explorer.

'What do *you* have to prove?' she asked.

He tilted his head back, an impossible to read expression on his face.

'The other day someone told me I wasn't quite the hero I thought I was.'

She stared at him, her heart suddenly pounding so hard against her ribs she thought the force of it might send her flying down the hillside.

Trying to play it cool, she held his gaze. 'Is that right?'

He nodded. 'Unfortunately, there's a major shortage of damsels in distress on the island, so I had to resort to rescuing sheep.'

Watching Frankie's lips curve up into one of those tree-felling smiles she seemed able to produce at will, Arlo felt his stomach go into freefall. He had slept badly again, woken early, and even though he'd felt exhausted his body had been twitchy, his mind too restless to let him even try falling back to sleep.

It was only as he'd walked downstairs that he'd realised why he was finding it so difficult to sleep. The storm was passing, any day now the causeway would be safe to cross, and Frankie Fox would be free to leave.

Yesterday morning he would have greeted that statement with relief. But a lot had changed in the twenty-four hours since he'd found her semi-naked in his bed—not least, his opinion of her.

His chest tightened. He hadn't expected her to do so, but she had impressed him yesterday. She'd worked hard, listened, and asked questions where necessary. In another life he might have given her a real job, or he might even have—

Have what?

He stopped mid-thought, but it made no difference. His body was already answering the question.

Gritting his teeth, he stared past her to where the waves were tumbling against the rocks. He had to get a grip. Frankie might not be the flaky little chancer he'd thought she was, but she was not his type.

For starters she was already involved in some way with Johnny, but even if she wasn't, she was only twenty-one—little more than a kid.

Except she hadn't kissed like a kid.

She'd kissed like a woman.

His shoulders tensed as he remembered the soft, breathy moans she'd made as his tongue had parted her lips. He'd wanted her, and he was pretty sure she had wanted him at that moment. But he'd tried living in the moment before, blindly trusting to what Frankie called 'planetary forces', and it had been an out-and-out disaster.

Only it was a lot easier to think that when Frankie wasn't actually standing in front of him, looking ridiculously swamped and yet frustratingly sexy in one of his old jackets.

Conscious of her gaze and needing to do something to shift the restless energy inside him, he swung the sheep down from his shoulders onto the grass. As it trotted away without a backward glance, he unwrapped his sweater from around his waist and pulled it over his head.

Heart beating fast, he glanced up at the sky. For the first time since he'd returned home there was a tiny patch of blue. By tomorrow, aside from the battered-looking gorse bushes, it would be as if the storm had never happened. The causeway would open. Life would go back to normal. Some parts of it, anyway.

He cleared his throat. 'By the way, you were right about Johnny. He did leave a message—two, actually—but they only came through yesterday evening. He said you needed to have some fun.'

But why? he wondered. She was young and beautiful, and she lived in London. Surely fun was at her fingertips.

Johnny had also said Frankie needed some TLC, but he didn't want to think about that. Not when the only kind of tender loving care he could think of offering her involved both of them naked and in his bed.

He looked down at her, not prompting, just waiting. She shrugged. 'Johnny's a good friend. He worries about me but I just needed a few days away from London. I feel fine now.'

She had chosen her words carefully but the sharp stab of relief he felt at hearing her describe Johnny as a friend was forgotten when he looked down at her.

Her mouth curved up at the corners, but there was something forced about the smile and he felt a prickle of guilt spread out across his skin. Unless TLC stood for total loss of control, he'd massively under-delivered.

'How could I not feel fine when I'm surrounded by all this?'

Now her smile seemed real, and some of the tension seemed to have left her face.

'You like it?'

She frowned at the surprise in his voice. 'Of course. It's beautiful. All nature's beautiful. It's so calming and uncomplicated.'

Smiling, he shook his head. 'Not all nature, I can assure you.'

'Are you talking about Antarctica?'

As she looked over at him, he saw a flicker of curiosity in her blue eyes.

'What's it like?'

It was a question he'd been asked so many times,

but for some reason he wanted to give her more than just a generic answer.

'It's exhausting. Terrifying. Intoxicating. And heartbreakingly beautiful. A lot of the time it feels like a dream.' He tilted his face upwards, towards the sky. 'Everything is so extreme out there. The sky is bigger, the wind is stronger, the cold is like nothing you've ever felt, and the sea is this beautiful endlessly changing blue...'

She looked over at him and he felt his heartbeat stumble.

Not as blue or as beautiful as Frankie's eyes.

Forcing his gaze away from her face, he stared down at the jagged rocks. 'There are icebergs there that are the size of countries. And the air...it has texture. You feel like you could scoop it up in your hands.'

Her face was flushed. 'It sounds amazing. But I guess it would have to be for you to want to leave this place so often.'

He gazed down at the chimney stacks of the Hall. Leaving the island, leaving his home, always filled him with sadness. He loved everything about it. But some things were more important than feelings—his or anyone else's. He'd learned that the hard way.

He hadn't always felt like that. As a child, his parents' adoration for each other had seemed like a mythical power. Only watching that power wither away during his mother's illness had been devastating, and his father's furious grief almost more so.

He should have realised then that it didn't matter what you felt or how strongly you felt it—the power of love was no match for cold, hard facts. But he had been young and desperate, and so, driven by an incoherent need to save an ideal, he'd impulsively married a woman he barely knew.

Now he understood that if you wanted to save something—someone—you needed more than feelings. In fact, feelings were just a distraction.

He shrugged. 'It's addictive. It demands so much of you. And yet in other ways it's so fragile. I think that's what makes it so incredible...unique. There's nowhere like it.' He felt her gaze on his face. 'But you don't need me to tell you about it. Go and see for yourself.'

'Me?'

'Why not? The poles aren't some snow-covered men-only club for boffins or billionaires with frozen beards and thousand-yard stares.'

She burst out laughing. 'Is that how you see yourself?'

It was disconcerting how much he liked making her laugh. 'More importantly, is that how you see me?'

The air between them seemed to thicken and he felt his body tense as she bit into her lip.

'You are a bit intense. But your beard isn't frozen.'

He shook his head. 'You know, having you around is doing wonders for my ego.'

She rolled her eyes. 'I don't think your ego needs bolstering.' Squinting up at the sky, she sighed. 'It's so lovely out here, but I suppose we'd better get back to work.'

For the briefest of moments his disappointment vied with his shock that work had slipped his mind, but then he nodded. 'Yes, we should.'

Constance had seen them coming and was waiting by the back door.

'Apparently the storm warning's been reduced to yellow,' she said. 'So, am I right to assume that this will be the last night of your stay with us, Frankie?'

A small silence bled into the hallway as Frankie glanced up not at Constance but at him.

Was it? Was it her last night?

But before he could open his mouth she said quietly, 'Yes. It's been lovely, but I have to get back to London and I would have been going back tomorrow, anyway. Nothing's changed.'

'No,' he agreed, holding her gaze. 'Nothing's changed at all.'

CHAPTER FIVE

PICKING UP HER LIP-LINER, Frankie stared at herself in the dressing table mirror. So this was it. Her last night at Hadfield Hall.

She couldn't quite believe it, but from the moment Constance had asked about her plans, time had done another of those contortions, so that in what felt like a matter of seconds the day was over and it was time to dress for dinner.

Her pulse quivered and, breathing out shakily, she gazed over to where her suitcase sat on the bed.

Nothing's changed.

Throughout the day, her words and Arlo's response had kept popping into her head. And she was right—they both were. Nothing had changed.

Only it felt as if something had. Actually, it felt as if *everything* had.

Oh, for goodness' sake.

Frowning, she smoothed over where she had jerked the lip pencil upwards. She took a breath. Maybe that was why, for one fleeting, truly idiotic moment, she had thought he was going to invite her to stay longer. Not that she would have accepted, of course. That would be utterly insane. Her flat, her job, her *life* was in London.

This was a lovely place to visit, and okay, she

and Arlo weren't at each other's throats anymore, but he was still a stranger.

A stranger she had kissed...

Refocusing with an effort, she glanced down at her cream cashmere jumper and dark red silk skirt, then lower to her high-heeled red shoes, trying to see herself as Arlo would.

But, really, what was the point?

Her pulse stilled. If there was one thing she'd learned about Arlo Milburn it was that it didn't pay to second-guess him.

He was already waiting for her in the dining room, standing by the fireplace looking down at the flames, one arm resting on the overmantel. Her breath seemed to spontaneously combust in her throat as he looked up at her, his grey eyes narrowing admiringly.

'You look beautiful.'

He was looking at her steadily, with total attention, and she felt her face and hands grow warm. 'I thought I'd make a bit of an effort.' She smiled, feeling suddenly shy. 'You look great too,' she added, her eyes skimming his dark trousers and a shirt that was so flawlessly white his upper body looked as if it was made of Arctic ice.

She wasn't just being polite. He really did look great. Both his trousers and shirt were cut beautifully and emphasised his muscular thighs and the wideness of his shoulders.

'Usually I wear this when I win something.' He didn't smile back. 'So it seemed appropriate.'

She frowned. 'What have you won?'

'Dinner with you, obviously,' he said quietly.

His words tingled like snowflakes against her skin. But of course, he was just being nice because she was leaving.

She smiled. 'Some people would probably see that as the consolation prize.'

He held out his hand. 'Not people worth knowing.'

He led her to her seat, and as she waited for him to sit down, she gazed around the room. She had spent such a short time here, but already everything felt so familiar...

Arlo felt so familiar.

Glancing over, she felt her throat constrict. He was changing before her eyes. That tense, angry man whose dark eyes had spilled scorn on her was now reaching over to fill her wine glass.

The food was superb again. Guinea fowl with leeks and morels followed a starter of roasted scallops with sea herbs, and to finish there was a white chocolate mousse with lemon sorbet. And although she'd been expecting the conversation to be a little stop-start, it wasn't at all. In fact, he was surprisingly good company. Intelligent, with that dry sense of humour she had glimpsed before, and happy to talk about practically anything.

Her pulse dipped. But no doubt he was just making an effort because it was her last night.

She laid down her spoon. 'That was wonderful, but I truly couldn't eat another thing.'

'Really?' He frowned. 'Only there's another two courses—'

She glanced up just in time to see the smile leaving his lips. 'Very funny.'

'Don't you mean *hashtag can't stop laughing*?' he said softly.

Now she was laughing and shaking her head. Then she groaned. 'Please don't make me laugh… it hurts too much.'

'Sorry.' He leaned back, studying her. 'You know, when Johnny and I ate too much when we were younger my dad used to take us up to the rumpus room and make us run races.'

'Is that the long room with all the little leaded windows?'

He nodded. 'The windows are like that so you can play ball games up there without smashing the glass. We used to play everything. Rugby, tennis…' His grey eyes met hers. 'Cricket?'

'No, absolutely not,' she said, shaking her head. 'I'm too full to run—and not in these heels. It wouldn't be a fair contest.'

In the light from the chandeliers his features didn't look so hard, so at odds with each other, as he held her gaze. 'If you keep those heels on, the disadvantage would be entirely mine.'

She felt her skin grow warm. 'What about a game of snooker?' she said quickly. She had spotted the table during yesterday's brief exploration. 'That shouldn't be too strenuous.'

'It's actually a billiard table,' he said as they walked into the wood-panelled room. 'Billiards is a great game, but most people treat it like the dull cousin of snooker and pool.'

'You mean like Mr Collins in *Pride and Prejudice*?'

He shook his head. 'No. Mr Collins *was* dull. Billiards is not. It's simple to learn, but it punishes you far more than snooker or pool when it comes to the fundamentals.'

She bit her lip. 'And that's important, is it? Punishing yourself?'

'Only in as much as it allows you to punish your opponent more,' he said softly.

Their eyes met and then he handed her a cue.

'Okay, then. The rules of the game: billiards is played with one red ball and two white cue balls...'

They agreed that the winner would be the first to reach a hundred points.

'That sounds like a lot,' she said slowly. 'But okay...'

Forty minutes later, Frankie leaned back against the table, biting into her lip.

Arlo laid his cue down on the baize. 'Frankie

Fox,' he said quietly. 'Social media influencer and stone-cold, red-hot billiard player.'

She screwed up her face. 'I was going to tell you, but—'

'You thought you'd wipe the floor with me instead?'

Her mouth dried up as he walked slowly towards her.

'No,' she protested. 'You just looked so sweet and serious when you were explaining everything. I couldn't bring myself to stop you.'

'Sweet?' He blew out a breath and then he smiled. 'That's a new one. So, who taught you how to play?'

'My brother Harry.' She blinked. It was probably the first time she had spoken her brother's name in more than eighteen months, and it scraped inside her mouth. Fixing a smile to her face, she continued, 'The pub down the road from where he lived at university had a billiard table. If it's any consolation, I used to beat him and all his friends too.'

Sighing, Arlo shook his head. 'I suppose I should be grateful we didn't play for money.'

'I don't want your money—'

He was standing so close she could feel his warm breath, could see the metallic gleam and the urgency in his eyes.

'What *do* you want?' he said slowly.

It was a simple question. The answer was not. She swallowed, shifted, transfixed by the clashing arcs and clefts of his features. It was like looking at a topographic map, and she wondered what would happen if she ran her finger along one of the lines.

Where would it lead her?

Her body was tingling, her heart hammering inside her chest. Everything looked and felt different—more *there*, more sensuous. The faint scent of woodsmoke…the billiard table pressing into her thighs…the shimmering chandeliers…

Maybe it was the wine, she thought. But she knew that it wasn't, and she felt something stir low down.

She knew that it was Arlo.

He was the answer. She wanted him.

Her insides tightened, the truth accelerating her racing pulse. But everything was tangled, snarled together so tightly that she was incapable of doing anything other than stand there and stare at him.

'I don't know,' she said at last.

He took a step closer. 'Would it help if I told you what I wanted?'

Her eyes found his. He was watching her intently, his face taut, the muscles in his arms bunching beneath his shirt.

'What do you want?' she whispered, clenching and unclenching her fists.

Reaching out, he ran his finger along her jaw. 'I want you. And you want me.'

The rawness in his voice shocked her so much

that she didn't even attempt to deny his words. His dark eyes were trained on her face and the tension inside her was at breaking point.

She knew that he was waiting for her, that he would walk away without a murmur if she wanted him too. But she didn't want him to. Only she couldn't seem to speak.

She took a breath and said the only word that would form in her mouth. 'Yes.'

He leaned into her, dipping his head so that his lips brushed against hers, and then his hands were pulling her closer, so that it felt as if they were starting where they'd left off last time.

Heart pounding, she slid her fingers over the solid muscles of his chest, almost dizzy with the freedom of touching him. His hands slid under her jumper to cup her breasts, and she moaned against his lips as the nipples hardened.

'Open your mouth,' he said hoarsely, and she responded, tightening her fingers around his arms as he deepened the kiss.

Only she wanted more and, pushing him back, she grabbed her sweater and pulled it over her head. His eyes narrowed as she began undoing his shirt, and then, with a growl of frustration, he yanked it apart, the buttons flying everywhere.

She swallowed hard as he dragged the sleeves down over his wrists, and then he was reaching out, pushing aside the fabric of her simple white bra. Her whole body tensed as his callused thumbs chafed against the taut tips of her breasts, and suddenly she was desperate to feel his mouth against them.

Moving her hands over the hard planes of his chest, she leaned towards him, arching forward, then gasped as his lips fastened on her breast.

She heard him grunt, and then he was lifting her onto the billiard table, pushing her skirt up. His thighs were between hers as he drew first one, then the other nipple into his mouth, his teeth scraping lightly over the rigid flesh.

She moaned weakly. It felt so good, so right... she'd had no idea it could feel like this. Hunger was surging through her and, sucking in a breath, she pressed her hand flat against the hard ridge of his erection.

Groaning, he lifted his head. His jaw was clenched, the muscles in his chest stretched tight.

'What is it? Is something wrong?' she asked.

Breathing out shakily, he shook his head. 'Nothing's wrong. It's just I haven't done this in a while.' He grimaced. 'I don't want it to be over before it's started.'

Her eyes dropped from the flushed skin of his torso, moved lower. Half-naked, fully aroused, he looked amazing.

She felt a rush of nerves.

And intimidating.

'Actually, I haven't done it in a while either,' she said slowly. 'In fact, not very much at all.'

He looked at her, eyes appraising her, and then he cleared his throat. 'But you have done it…?'

'I'm not a virgin,' she said quickly. 'Why? Did you think I was?'

His fingers tensed. 'Yes, just now…but only because I thought by "not very much" you meant not at all.'

'I don't want you to be disappointed.'

He was breathing deeply, his chest rising and falling, a dark flush in his cheekbones. Reaching up, he cupped her chin, his grey gaze skimming over her throat, her collarbone, her breasts…

'Listen to me, Frankie, you do not disappoint.'

Her belly clenched as he brushed the thumb across her lips.

'And, just for the record, it's my job to satisfy you—not the other way round.'

She felt wetness between her thighs, and she dragged in a strangled breath as he dropped to his knees and kissed his way down her body, his roughened hands stroking her until she shook with need.

She didn't remember it being like this. He made her want him so much.

Gently, he pushed her legs open, dipping his fingers into her slick heat, and then she felt his warm breath on the skin of her thighs as he parted her with his tongue.

Her head fell back, and she swayed, her fingers

tightening around the lip of the table. Heat flared inside her and she dragged in another breath, trying to clear the dizziness from her head.

But his tongue was relentless.

Teasing, taking, tasting.

No one had ever touched her like this.

She felt helpless and hungry. His touch was dissolving her, the pleasure building as his hands slid under her bottom and he raised her up to meet his mouth.

The ball of heat inside her was pulsing in time with his tongue and her hands caught in his hair, holding him steady. She was lifting herself up, the pleasure tipping almost into pain as she rocked faster and faster, and then she spasmed, muscles tightening, tensing...

Heart thudding, she held on to him as he stood up, his eyes finding hers. Her hand slid over his stomach to the buckle of his belt, freeing him before she wrapped her hand around his hard length.

His breath hitched. 'Turn round,' he said hoarsely, and she felt a ripple of need shiver across her skin.

His hands gripped her waist and she braced herself, head spinning, as his lips trailed down her neck. She heard the sound of something being torn and dazedly realised that she had been too caught up in her climax to remember a condom.

He pushed into her slowly, his breath vibrating

against her throat, and then he reached round her to cup her breasts as he started to move.

Her belly clenched as his hand moved to her clitoris, and she felt him accelerate in time to the second climax building inside her. Then he tensed, groaning, his big body engulfing her, his head falling against her shoulder.

For a moment he lay against her, breathing raggedly. and then he pulled back. Glancing down, she saw herself as he did. Skirt rucked up about her waist, bare legs, high heels...

Her breath caught. She felt stunned. She had never done anything like that before. Never felt what he had made her feel.

'I...' she said, searching for words. But there were none.

Their eyes met, and his gaze sent flickers of feeling everywhere.

Was this—? Should they—? Did he—?

She had loved how his body felt on hers, and she was suddenly desperate to touch him. Only she knew that if she touched him it would start up again, and that might ruin everything. This was enough. It had to be enough.

Leaning down, she scooped up her jumper and pulled it over her head. 'I should probably go up now. I've got to pack.'

He stared at her, tall, silent, his eyes dark, his face expressionless.

'Then I'll let you go,' he said.

It was the right thing to do. The only thing to do. But it took every ounce of willpower she had to walk past him into the dark corridor.

CHAPTER SIX

IT WAS GOING to be a beautiful day, Frankie thought, gazing out of the car window.

In London, she never really noticed the weather, except in terms of whether she could legitimately take a taxi. In fact, she was pretty sure she'd never even listened to a weather forecast.

But up here in Northumberland she found it mesmerising. It was like watching a magic show. One moment the sky was conjuring up flocks of grey clouds, like sheep, the next streaks of sunlight that pierced the grey like shimmering, iridescent ribbons.

Right now, the clouds were growing wispier by the minute, while on either side of the causeway the waves jostled one another half-heartedly before turning to foam.

Her pulse shivered. It was hard to believe this was the same sea that had almost swept her off the causeway. Hard, too, to believe that she was going home.

Taking a breath, she glanced furtively to where Arlo sat beside her, his large, powerful hands resting with deceptive languor on the steering wheel, his eyes fixed on the cobbled road.

She felt her body tense. Was he thinking the

same thing? Or was he just counting down the minutes until they reached the train station?

Her heartbeat accelerated as she remembered the moment last night when he had leaned forward and kissed her. She'd told herself that their first kiss had been a one-off and that Arlo wasn't her type.

But everything she'd told herself had been wrong.

Everything she'd known about sex had been wrong too.

She'd only done it twice before. Both with her ex, Aidan. The first time had been just awkward, and a little uncomfortable. The second had been better in terms of comfort, but afterwards she had wondered what all the fuss was about.

Now she knew.

Last night with Arlo had been a revelation. *He* had been a revelation.

As his lips had fused with hers it had been like flint striking rock. Everything inside her had been flame and heat. His body had felt so solid, so strong, and as she'd pressed against him, she'd had the sudden intense feeling that she wanted to stay in his arms for ever...

She pressed her hands together in her lap.

It wasn't just intense—it was crazy.

And yet it had been so tempting...

To take it a step further.

To go with him upstairs and do it again, and again, and again...

But something had held her back—some sixth sense that had told her if she went further, she would soon be out of her depth. She'd already gone further than she probably should have.

Arlo obviously felt the same way.

He parked and had her suitcase out of the boot before she'd even taken off her seat belt. Clearly, he couldn't wait to get rid of her, she thought as she struggled to keep up with his pavement-eating stride.

'All right, Mr Milburn. I thought you only just got back. Where you going this time, then?'

'I'm not going anywhere, Alan.' Arlo's face uncreased fractionally as he shook hands with the uniformed station attendant. 'I'm just dropping Ms Fox off. Okay if I see her onto the train?'

'That's really not—' she began.

But Arlo was already walking swiftly along the platform, her now-battered suitcase clamped under his arm. Trailing behind, she followed him into a carriage, heart thumping as she watched him push her case into the overhead luggage rack.

'Okay, then.' His eyes were as expressionless as his voice. 'Have a good trip.'

Her heart lurched. *Was that it?*

But before she even had a chance to open her mouth he turned and walked away, the hem of his coat curling around his legs like the tail of a panther.

Her head was suddenly pounding so hard that it hurt to stand, and for one horrible moment she thought she might faint. Forcing her feet to move, she sat down in the nearest seat even as somewhere inside her head she heard her own voice telling Arlo that she'd never passed out in her life.

Pressing her head against the window, she closed her eyes. Last night had been an admission of something beyond thought—the raw and inescapable hunger that seemed to have engulfed them both since that moment on the causeway.

It had been a moment of passion. A moment, not even a night. Only something had happened. Something had passed between them...

The carriage doors opened.

'I think she's got a cheek, talking to you like that.' The woman's voice floated over her head. 'You should tell Mary. She'd give her what for—'

'I don't want to cause any trouble...' A second woman, quieter, anxious sounding.

'Frankie.'

The deep voice made her eyes snap open and, turning her head, she froze.

Arlo was standing beside her, his broad, muscular body effortlessly filling the carriage, his face austere and irregular beneath the harsh overhead lights.

She stared up at him wordlessly, her skin prickling with shock. He looked almost as stunned as she did, as if he wasn't quite sure what he was doing.

'Is this how you want to leave things?' he asked.

There was short, quivering silence as she stared at him wordlessly, stunned by the directness of his question.

'No.' Breathing out shakily, she shook her head. 'No, it's not.'

Something flared in his dark eyes and then he was reaching up and pulling down her suitcase. 'Then come with me.'

This was not something he did, Arlo thought as he reversed out of the parking space and accelerated away from the car park. He did not chase after women and drag them off trains. It was a mistake on so many levels. He knew that logically and unequivocally—and yet here he was doing it.

It had taken two minutes.

Two minutes of his legs carrying his numb body forward before he had turned and headed back to the station past an open-mouthed Alan. And with each step he'd told himself that he could stop, turn around, go back to the car at any point.

But as soon as he stepped into the carriage and seen her sitting there that had changed. He'd spoken before he'd caught up with himself, the question fully formed on his lips, and by the time he'd considered the bigger picture they were walking back, past Alan.

The horse had well and truly bolted.

Or rather the train had left the station.

Maybe Frankie hadn't considered the consequences until now either. It would certainly explain her silence, he thought, staring fixedly out through the windscreen.

He was still staring fixedly ahead as they strode back into the Hall, past an open-mouthed Constance and upstairs.

The enormity, the incredible stupidity of what he was doing, hit him like a wrecking ball as he walked into Frankie's bedroom. At the station he had simply wanted to stop her leaving. That had been the endpoint. Now, though, he saw it was just the beginning.

Only of what?

Last night he had behaved recklessly, driven by a compulsion he hadn't understood. But in some part of what could loosely be called his brain it had made sense. He had wanted Frankie, wanted to satisfy the hunger that had been eating at him ever since he'd found her in his bed.

If she hadn't wanted him he would have walked away, of course. Only she *had* wanted him. She had turned to flame beneath his fingers and now his body was hard and aching for more.

He didn't know why. All he knew was that they weren't finished. And that it was the pursuit of their unfinished connection that had brought them here.

'There's another train in four hours.' Still holding her suitcase, he swung round to face her. 'If you've changed your mind about coming back.'

'I haven't,' she said quietly.

There was a short, stiff pause and Arlo felt his chest tighten. This was exactly the kind of conversation he hated. Taut, emotional, unpredictable... But, if anything, Frankie seemed even more uncomfortable with it than he did, so that he was more concerned with putting her at ease.

'It felt wrong...you leaving like that.'

Her eyes found his. 'I felt the same. It's just that nothing like this...' she swallowed '...like *us*, has ever happened to me before.'

His heartbeat was drumming inside his head. Nothing like this...*like her*...he thought silently, had happened to him either.

Looking down at her, he felt his shoulders tense. He had nothing to offer her in the long term. Even the idea of permanence induced in him a kind of vertigo, and he needed her to know that.

His eyes found hers. 'I don't do relationships, but I think we have something special. Something I'd like to explore.'

He held his breath. No polar region had ever excited him as much as the idea of exploring every inch of Frankie.

'So when do we start?' she asked.

She hadn't moved, but the room suddenly felt smaller. She seemed closer, and she was breathing as unevenly as he was.

Arlo stared at her in silence, her words turning his groin painfully hard. This was why he'd gone after her: sex. Only it was more than sex. When he looked at Frankie there was fire, heat and hunger on a level he couldn't remember feeling before—not even for Harriet.

His throat felt as if it was clogged with his hot, wet breath, and he was holding his body so tautly it felt as if it might snap.

A minute went by, then another, and then they both moved at the same time—his hand wrapping around her waist and pulling her closer as she leaned forward, her fingers sliding over his shoulders.

As her lips parted against his he forgot to breathe. Her mouth was hot, and the taste of her was making his head swim. Shifting closer, he deepened the kiss, her soft moan instantly taking him to the point where kissing was not enough.

She clearly thought the same.

He could feel her fingers tugging clumsily at the sleeves of his coat, and without breaking the kiss he unzipped the front of her jacket, pushing it off her shoulders and down her arms.

Now her hands were on his chest, pulling at his jumper.

'Easy, Frankie.' He caught her arms, his eyes

finding hers. 'We have time. We have plenty of time.'

'Okay…' Her fingers bit into his arm and she began pulling him towards the bed. 'But let's just get undressed…'

Her words were like petrol thrown on a bonfire.

Turning, he pushed the door shut and began to yank his jumper over his head. His T-shirt followed hers onto the floor, and then they both kicked off their boots and socks.

Now they were both just wearing jeans.

Dragging his eyes from the swell of her breasts, he drew her closer, his lips finding hers, and then he kissed her—kissed her until she moaned, and he felt her body start to soften.

Head spinning, he nudged her backwards. As they toppled onto the bed he pulled her on top, so that she was straddling him. Her hands were everywhere, sliding over the skin of his back and shoulders and down his arms, as if she couldn't quite believe he was real.

He understood that feeling. He couldn't believe she was real…that he was free to kiss and touch her…

Capturing her face in his hands, he teased her top lip with his tongue. He wanted more. He needed more. He needed all of her. *Everything*.

Reaching up, he touched her small breasts, cupping them in his hands, grazing his thumbs over the nipples, and then he sucked one tautened tip into his mouth, feeling it swell against his tongue.

Her head fell back and his body tensed as she began to squirm restlessly against him, against where he was growing harder by the minute. He sat up and, using the muscles of his thighs, tipped her forward onto the heavy press of his erection.

Frankie breathed out shakily.

He was very hard and very big.

Heart thudding, she reached up to touch his face, her fingers moving lightly against his beard-roughened jaw.

'I didn't say it last night, but you don't disappoint either,' she said softly.

Abruptly he leaned forward and, wrapping his hand in her hair, lifted her face to his and kissed her—a hard, hungry, open-mouthed, searing kiss that stole the breath from her lungs so suddenly that her head was spinning and she was shaking...

A moan that seemed to come from the hot, molten core of her body rose up in her throat and she rocked against him, her fingers sliding through his hair.

He grunted, and in one motion grabbed her arms and rolled her onto the bed, unbuttoning her jeans and tugging them down her legs, taking her panties with them.

For a moment he just stood at the end of the bed, watching her, face taut, jaw clenched tight, muscles bunched, eyes dark with an undisguised hunger that sent flickers of excitement scampering over her skin.

And then he was pulling off his jeans and boxer shorts.

It was the first time she'd seen him completely naked.

Her mouth felt as if it had been sandblasted. He definitely didn't disappoint, she thought, sucking in a sharp breath.

Then suddenly he was on the bed beside her, pulling her into his arms.

Breathing shakily, she ran her hands over the hard, defined muscles of his chest, her fluttering fingers tracing the line of dark hair down his stomach.

A shiver of need ran through her as she took him in her hand.

Then leaning into him, she drew up her leg, to meet the blunt tip of his erection. He jerked against her, a raw sound breaking from his lips, and, reaching past her, shook his wallet from the back pocket of his jeans.

Pulse quivering, she watched him unwrap the condom and slide it onto his hard length, and then his dark eyes locked with hers as he pushed gently against her.

'Is that okay?'

'Yes.' She breathed out slowly, opening her legs

wider, then wider still. 'Yes, like that. Yes,' she said again, curling her hands around his shoulders.

He was pushing up inside her, his hand lifting her bottom so that there was nothing between them but heat and sweat, his thumb stroking her clitoris as she moved. His dark eyes locked with hers and she cried out, her body tensing in release, and then he was thrusting hard into her, pulling her close and burying his face against her throat.

For a moment he lay on top of her, breathing shakily, and then, lifting himself from her body, he rolled off her and got to his feet.

His eyes scudded down her body then back up to her face. 'I'll be right back.'

She stared after him, savouring the broad expanse of his back and the muscular curve of his shoulders. He was so unashamedly male, and she felt so unashamedly satisfied.

She shivered. Without the warmth of his body, she felt cold. Shifting backwards up the bed, she wriggled under the covers.

Moments later he slid in beside her, pulling her against him.

She let her hand rest lightly across his stomach, feeling calmer than she had for weeks…maybe months. Coming back had felt like a risk, but maybe this was what she'd needed all along. Intimacy. Physical contact.

She had read in a magazine that hugging someone produced feel-good hormones, and sex was the most intense kind of hugging. That must be why she felt so good.

Only nothing this good ever lasted.

'Don't overthink it.'

Startled, Frankie looked up. Arlo was staring down at her, his grey eyes steady and unblinking.

'What just happened—don't overthink it,' he said quietly. 'It's not that complicated.'

Isn't it?

She stared at him, a beat of panic pulsing over her skin. Maybe not for him. He could just lie back and enjoy the aftermath of release. But feeling calm and happy carried a different risk for her.

'I'm not overthinking,' she lied.

She let her hair fall forward to hide her face. It wasn't a complete lie, more a half-truth. But she wasn't ready to tell him the whole truth.

'Frankie, look at me.'

His voice was impossible to ignore. Lifting her head, she met his gaze.

'Look, I haven't had a day off in a long time and you need a break,' he said. 'We're just going to spend it together.'

Her heart missed a beat.

Could she? Should she?

But she'd already answered both those questions by coming back. And Arlo wasn't offering something solid or permanent—something that could be lost or broken. It wasn't a contract of commitment. What they had, what they both wanted, was purely physical. So why not let it run its course?

'I'd like that.'

'I'd like that too,' he said, his dark eyes locking with hers.

She felt her body start to melt. It was lucky, she thought, that she didn't have feelings for Arlo. To love a man who made you feel this way would be terrifying.

But then his head dipped, and he pulled her against him, and she stopped thinking and surrendered to a wave of want and need and heat...

Frankie had been slightly worried about facing Constance again, but as it turned out Frankie was not the only person who had returned to the island. Throughout the day more and more staff kept arriving.

Arlo seemed amused by her astonishment. 'What did you think? That Constance did everything on her own?'

She had. But now she thought about it, it seemed ridiculously obvious that that would be impossible. The house was vast, and then there were the gardens, and the island itself...

'There are twelve people working here full-time.'

'What? Even when you're not here?'

He nodded. 'Most of the staff have been here for at least a decade. They're like family.'

Frankie smiled, but inside she felt that familiar ache of loss and envy at the word family. Only she had no right to envy the very thing she had helped destroy, she thought, as Arlo introduced her to Constance's team of indoor staff.

'You can meet everyone else later,' he said as they left the kitchen. 'This way.'

He touched her lightly on the back and she felt a flicker of heat low in her belly. 'Where are we going?'

'Nero needs a run. I thought we could go down to the beach.' His dark gaze rested on her face. 'Work up an appetite.'

It was glorious outside.

The sky was an almost Mediterranean blue, and the tide was out, and to her amazement the beach was sandy. Arlo rolled his eyes as she pulled off her boots and socks, but then he did the same.

'Oh, it's freezing!' She gasped as the sea swirled over her bare feet. But only for a moment. Then it was still cold, but in a good way. 'It's so beautiful,' she said, gazing down the beach. 'It actually makes my heart beat faster.'

Arlo picked up a stick and hurled it a ridiculous distance down the beach. 'Are you sure that isn't me?'

Reaching down herself, she flicked some cold water at him and then started to run. He caught her easily, pulling her against him so that she felt suddenly breathless with his nearness.

'You are going to pay for that, Ms Fox.'

'Big talk, Mr Milburn.'

He laughed then—a genuine laugh that made her go weak in the middle.

'That feels like a challenge,' he said.

She laughed. 'Is that your way of saying you want a billiards rematch? Because we can play for money this time, if you want.'

'Only if you wear those shoes.' He smiled slowly. '*Just* those shoes.'

The slow burn of his gaze reached inside her, pressing down against her pelvis. 'I'm game if you are.'

Grimacing, he shook his head. 'You know, your brother has a lot to answer for. I think at some point I'm going to have a few words with him about unleashing you with a cue on an unsuspecting male population.'

Feeling cold on the inside, she stared past him at the sea.

Answer him. Say something...anything, she told herself.

But her mouth wouldn't move.

After a short, gritty pause, he said slowly, 'It's not a big thing, Frankie. I'm not angling to meet your family.'

She felt her chest pull tight with anger and panic.

How dare he throw that at her? This was his fault. If he'd warned her that he was going to start talking about her family she would have prepared herself.

'Not everything is about you, Arlo—' she snapped.

Adrenaline was spiking inside her and her hands were shaking. She could feel it building beneath her skin. The misery. The guilt. The memories she fought so hard to keep at bay. Her heart twisted and she pressed her knuckles against the ache.

'Frankie...'

His voice was gentle—too gentle. It was melting her anger, melting the barriers she had built, so that the memories were filling her head and the truth was spilling from her lips.

'You can't meet my brother.' Tears filled her eyes. 'You can't meet any of my family. They died in an accident two years ago. They all died. Everyone except me.'

For a few half-seconds Arlo stared down at Frankie in shock and horror, and then he pulled her into his arms, holding her close until she softened against him just as he had on that first morning.

Only this was so much worse.

'It's okay, Frankie. It's okay,' he said, holding her tighter.

But obviously it wasn't.

His heart was thudding painfully hard, the last

few days replaying on fast-forward inside his head. The things he'd said, the way he'd acted.

'Here.' Pulling out a handkerchief, he gently wiped her eyes and cheeks.

She bit into her lip. 'I'm sorry. You don't need to deal with all this. It's not fair. You lost your parents too.'

He tensed. They hadn't talked about his parents, Lucien and Helena, but no doubt Johnny had told her the basics—that his mother had died young and their father was dead now too. Heaviness was seeping through his chest. He'd known pain and loss, but to lose everyone like that... It was impossible to imagine how that must have felt—how it must still feel, given that it was so recent.

'You don't need to worry about that. I've got strong shoulders.'

He pulled her closer. She needed to talk, but he felt as if he'd cornered her into the conversation, and he sensed that it would be easier for her to answer yes/no questions.

'Was it the same accident that gave you your scar?'

She nodded. 'It was a plane crash. We were coming back from a holiday in France. My dad was flying the plane.' Her mouth trembled. 'He loved medicine but flying was his passion.'

'Do you know what happened?'

He felt her shiver.

'Not really. At the inquest they said he'd fallen

asleep. I'd taken a travel sickness pill. The first thing I remember is waking up to this enormous headache.'

Arlo nodded mechanically, but inside his head he was visualising the scene. The wreckage. The bodies. The silence. His chest squeezed tight.

'Does Johnny know?' He hadn't consciously intended to ask that question, but for some reason he cared enormously about the answer.

She shook her head. 'I haven't really told anyone. I did a couple of sessions with a therapist, but I don't know how to tell people. It's stupid, really. I did try a few times, but they were always so horrified, and then I just ended up trying to make them feel better.'

It wasn't stupid. After his mother's death people had wanted to be kind, but mostly he'd found himself having to manage *their* reaction. The idea of Frankie trying to cope with that as well as everything else made the muscles in his arms tighten painfully.

Her eyes found his. 'You're a good listener,' she said quietly, sifting a layer of sand between her toes.

He pulled her closer and kissed her. Holding her, feeling her soft body against his, made his heart contract.

But he ignored it.

This wasn't about him. It was about Frankie. And she needed more than a few days off. She needed someone to fill the family-sized gap in her life. She needed someone to love her and look out for her.

He couldn't do any of those things but he could, and would, take care of her, for now, until it was time for her to leave.

CHAPTER SEVEN

HANDS TIGHTENING AGAINST the ship's wheel, Frankie squinted through the sunlight at the sea, her heartbeat leapfrogging in time to the waves.

She had not been prepared for this. For any of it.

For the patches of shining brightness or the dazzle of spray hitting the bow of the boat. But most of all for where the pursuit of her unfinished connection with Arlo Milburn had taken her.

They were on board his yacht, *The Aeolus*, and she couldn't quite believe that she was here with him.

Remembering her stumbling confession out on the beach, she felt her chest tighten. She still didn't really understand how she had ended up telling Arlo about the accident. She hadn't planned on telling him anything.

Why would she?

They'd promised one another nothing.

But Arlo had been so calm, unfazed—and in a way that wasn't surprising, given how he lived. He must have had to deal with far more terrifying things in Antarctica.

What she hadn't expected was for him to show compassion. Had she thought about it, she would have assumed he would be brisk, practical, detached. Instead, his gentleness had caught her off-guard, and she had been telling the truth when she'd said he was a good listener. He was the first person who had given her space to find the right words. Or maybe to realise that there *were* no right words.

He hadn't just rushed in and tried to fill the void with his pity and shock, and crucially he hadn't made it about him. And that was the most incredible part, given that he had lost both his parents too.

He had understood that in that moment there had been no room for his experiences, even though they were relevant. He was the first person who had seemed to know that she was in a dark place and that what she needed most of all was for him just to join her there.

So instead of telling her that he knew how she was feeling, or giving her advice, or trying to be positive, he had let her talk. He had listened—really listened—so that it had been easy to tell him the truth.

Her stomach muscles tightened. Not all of it—not the fact that she had caused the accident…that it was her fault that her family had died.

Just for a moment or two she had thought about it. A part of her had wanted to tell him. But she had tried telling the truth before in France, first at the hospital, with the *gendarmes*, and then again at the inquest, but both times it had made no difference.

She allowed herself a brief glance at the man

with the intense focus and formidable craggy profile at the other end of the boat.

At the hospital she'd thought it was because she was speaking English and that something had got lost in translation. But at the inquest there had been a translator, and it was then that she'd realised it wouldn't matter what language she was speaking, because telling the truth couldn't change what had happened.

It was her punishment not to be heard or understood, for to be understood would mean to be forgiven, and she didn't deserve that. And that was why she hadn't told Arlo about the part she'd played in the accident.

'Bear off a touch.'

Arlo's level voice came to her across the deck, and she looked over to where he was working the boat with the crew. She knew nothing about sailing, but it hadn't taken more than ten minutes at sea for her to understand that Arlo knew a lot.

Her pulse beat in her throat.

Like the rest of the crew he was wearing a dark T-shirt and buff-coloured chinos, but he still stood out from everyone.

Partly that was his height and breadth, but the human race had evolved sufficiently not to blindly follow someone simply on account of their strong thighs and wide shoulders. There was something else that drew her gaze. Something not actually visible. A certainty and authority that was both self-contained yet infinitely subtly responsive to those around him. An energy that thrummed from his core…that was tangible with your eyes shut. Or in the darkness of a bedroom.

Her face felt suddenly hot. She stared, dry-mouthed, her heart thumping against her ribs.

His hair was blowing in front of his eyes and her breath caught as he raised his hand and pushed it back from his angular face…

Their skin might be callused, and he might have lost the tips of two of his fingers, but she loved his hands. Their shape, their size, the dark hairs on the back of his wrists… They were so expressive of his mood, moving constantly while he spoke.

Watching them now, as he demonstrated something with a rope to one of the crew, she felt almost dizzy with hunger, remembering how they had moved over her body.

As if sensing her gaze, Arlo looked up. She felt her face grow warm as their eyes met, and then her heartbeat accelerated as he excused himself and began walking towards her.

'Everything okay?'

He'd stopped in front of her and, gazing up at him she felt a hum of pleasure. If not for the presence of the crew, she would have reached up and pulled his mouth onto hers.

'Yes, everything's fine.' She glanced past him to where the huge white sails swelled in the wind.

'Actually, it's incredible. But then I've only ever been on a ferry before, so…'

That morning, when Arlo had rather offhandedly suggested they go out on his boat, she had imagined some kind of dinghy, maybe even something with oars, but certainly nothing like this.

At over sixty metres long, *The Aeolus* was no rowing boat. She was a single-masted sloop-rigged superyacht. Although, truthfully, the expensively smooth contours reminded her less of a boat and more of a huge white gull—the kind Arlo had sketched out on the ice floes.

The Aeolus moved like a bird too, skimming fluidly and silently over the waves, following some invisible flight path that seemed to have more to do with the natural rhythms of the wind and the sea than the actions of the crew scurrying about the deck or the high-tech navigation system.

His dark gaze rested on her face. 'Well, they both float,' he said drily. 'But it's a bit like comparing a mule to a steeplechaser.'

She laughed. 'I wasn't actually comparing them.' A warm feeling settled in her stomach. His mood seemed lighter today, his gaze less shuttered, so that without giving it much thought she asked, 'So who taught you to sail?'

For a moment he didn't reply, and she wondered why. It wasn't exactly a contentious question. But then she realised that he wasn't weighing up his answer, but how much to say.

A bit like me, she thought, confused by this sudden small connection between them.

'My Great-Uncle Philip,' he said finally. 'He was in the navy. He loved sailing and—' his mouth flicked up into one of those stiff, almost-smiles '—he expected his entire family to love it too.'

He glanced past her to where the sails arced, winglike, above the unbelievably dark blue water.

'He had a beautiful boat. But before he'd let you on board you used to have to go out with him in a dinghy—prove yourself ready and worthy.'

Frankie shuddered. 'Like a test?'

He gave another of those careful almost-smiles. 'Exactly. It was pretty stressful. He was exacting, and relentless when it came to attention to detail, but he wanted you to be the best sailor you could be, and he thought that experience was a gift to share. It wasn't all hard work. We had a lot of good times too,' he said, almost as an afterthought. 'We'd sail all day and then we'd go back to the house, and the whole family would be there, and we'd have this huge meal, and me and my cousins would get to stay up late...'

Her throat tightened with a mix of pain and envy. She missed her family so much it felt as if someone was squeezing her chest in a vice. And yet she liked hearing Arlo talk about his family. It made his face change, grow handsome, almost...

Glancing up, she found him watching her and, feeling suddenly self-conscious, she said quickly,

'I don't think any boat could be as beautiful as *The Aeolus*. I feel like I'm in *The Great Gatsby*, or something, but she's not vulgar. There's something organic about how she looks…as if she's in harmony with the sea.'

He looked pleased, and she felt something wobble inside her. She didn't know why, but she liked watching his grey eyes lighten at something she'd said.

'You like her?' he asked.

'I do.' She nodded slowly, then frowned. 'Why are boats always female?'

He thought for a moment. 'Historically, I think it's because a lot of boats used to be named after women. *The Aeolus* isn't, so I don't know why I say "she" and "her". I suppose I'm a little traditional.'

Tilting her head to make his eyes meet hers, she smiled slightly. 'I wouldn't say that.'

There was a beat of silence as their gazes locked and she felt a shiver run over her skin, knowing that he, like her, was picturing the many and various ways they had made love last night—some of which she hadn't even known existed, all of which had made her forget how to breathe.

Her breath caught now as he took a step forward, moving behind her so that she could feel the press of his body, slipping his hands past her waist to close over her hands.

'What are you doing?'

'You were drifting,' he said softly.

His skin and the bristles of his beard were cold against her heated face and she felt her heartbeat lose its rhythm.

'I'm just correcting your course.'

It wasn't just the boat that was drifting, she thought helplessly. She could feel her body melting, her insides turning liquid and hot, limbs softening and if he hadn't been holding her she would have slid to the floor.

'I don't know where we're heading,' she said hoarsely.

In her head, she'd meant literally—as in their destination—only it had sounded different when she'd said the words out loud.

Her heart bumped against her ribs.

It was something they hadn't discussed—how and when this would end. When they were in bed, with her body still ringing like a tuning fork and his body so warm and solid next to hers, it had been easy to do as he said and not 'overthink' things.

So don't start now, she told herself. *Stop thinking about what you told him yesterday and just enjoy the ride.*

'I meant with the boat,' she said quickly.

There was a short, pulsing silence, and then slowly he raised his head and drew her chin around, so that she was looking at him. His face was completely expressionless.

'We're going to drop anchor just up the coast.

Constance has fixed us some lunch, and I thought you might enjoy a picnic on dry land. Or we can just stay on *The Aeolus*.' His fingers softened against her skin. 'But it's your call. Just tell me what you want, and I'll make it happen.'

Frankie had chosen a picnic, as he'd known she would, Arlo thought, glancing up at the flawless forget-me-not-blue sky.

Who wouldn't want a picnic on a day like this?

As if trying to make amends for the storm-force winds and slanting rain of a few days ago, the weather was perfect. Just the shimmering sun and a soft, Gulf-Stream-warmed breeze that barely lifted Frankie's dark red curls from her face.

A part of him was still reeling from her revelation yesterday. He hated to think that she'd been so hurt and lost, that she was still hurting.

That was what today was about.

Distracting her from the pain and hoping that it eased a little in the meantime—just like when Johnny had been teething and Arlo had carried him around the Hall, showing him the paintings in the early hours of the morning.

They had dropped anchor near one of the small uninhabited islands on the outer Firth of Forth. They'd taken the tender between the jagged rocks, and now they were sprawled on rugs on the heather-topped cliffs, picking through Constance's peerless picnic.

A loaf of homemade bread and a simple cold dish of thinly sliced slivers of chicken breast, dressed with a refreshing yoghurt sauce, were joined by baby beetroot with chutney, spiced aubergines, and some superb cheeses. To follow there was a rhubarb fool and a fruit and marzipan panforte, accompanied by a chilled bottle of Mâcon Blanc.

'I can't...' Frankie protested as he leaned forward and filled up her glass.

'On the contrary—you can. I'm the one who can't.' He dropped the bottle back in the ice bucket.

She screwed up her face. 'But that's not fair. You organised all of this and now you have to stay sober.'

Arlo stared at her in silence, a pulse ticking below his skin. It didn't matter that most of his crew were experienced sailors, or that it was a beautiful calm day. Alcohol and boats didn't mix.

But that didn't mean he was sober. On the contrary, being with Frankie made him feel as if he'd drunk a cellar full of wine. Although probably that was just the ozone. After a day at sea, he often felt that way. It was just a coincidence that he was here with her.

His heart thumped against his ribs.

He couldn't deny, though, that he liked knowing he could make her happy. That it was in his power to make her happy.

And unhappy.

Here, out in the sunlight, basking in Frankie's smile, it felt suddenly more important than ever to remember that—to remember how it had ended the last time he'd sought out that power.

He felt a twinge of guilt, as he always did when he thought about his blink-and-you'd-miss-it marriage.

His marriage…the divorce.

Harriet was part of a past he'd intentionally buried deep, deep down, so that he didn't have to think about it. And it had been working just fine until Frankie had arrived with *her* past, and *her* questions, and now suddenly memories kept pushing to the surface.

He gritted his teeth. Not just memories. Feelings too. Only it was going to stop now. Whatever it was he was feeling for Frankie had nothing to do with the past.

She needed a friend. It didn't mean anything. All he was doing was trying to make a few days of her life feel like a picnic. There was nothing more to it than that.

'I've been meaning to ask—what are the other rules?'

He glanced up at her. 'Rules?'

She waved her fork in the air. 'The other day you said that when you came home you had to eat real food at a table because that was one of your rules.'

Had he said that? How unbelievably pompous of him. He didn't have any rules.

Or rather he did. Unfortunately, he had broken both of them for Frankie.

His chest tightened. She wasn't the first woman he'd dated since Harriet, but with those other women he'd always been, if not happy, then ready and willing to part company after one night. And he'd never taken them home. Those were his unspoken rules.

But not only had he spent more than one night with Frankie, she was also staying at the Hall.

Sleeping in his bed.

An image of her as she'd looked that morning, pale limbs sprawled against the sheets, whipped at his senses and he felt a mix of resentment and relief at his ever-present hunger.

Feeling her gaze on his face, he shrugged. 'Nothing that exciting, I'm afraid. Just what everyone tells themselves after being on their own in a cold, brutal world. You know...the usual rules about not taking things, people, for granted.'

He'd said the first thing that came into his head but, glancing over at her pale, set face, he suddenly wished he had told her the truth. Silence stretched away from him, sweeping down to the sea like the great, granite cliff, and he swore softly.

'Frankie...' Reaching out, he took her hand. 'I didn't mean to—'

'It's fine.' Her fingers tightened around his. 'I know you weren't talking about me, but you're right.' She glanced down, her dark lashes fanning out over her cheeks. 'We all take so much for granted. I know I did.'

His heart squeezed at the bruised ache in her voice. That was the difference between them. She couldn't control her pain. She hadn't learned how to block it out. But then it was all so new for her.

'It's a problem most humans have,' he said slowly.

Before his mother's illness he had taken so much for granted. He felt his chest tighten, remembering those days out on his great-uncle's boat. They had been long, tiring days, but being surrounded by his family every hour he had felt magical, blessed. Bulletproof.

It was hard to believe now, but back then he had genuinely thought that they were invulnerable, that his parents' all-consuming love offered them some magical protection against hurt and injustice— even illness and death.

It hadn't helped that the bohemian world they'd created had felt so far removed from 'normal' life. The life lived by his cousins and his friends from school.

Nobody else's mother played her cello on the beach. His friends' fathers didn't let their sons have a day off school to practise making the perfect martini.

In their enchanted cocoon of love and laughter, anything 'real', like letters from the hospital, had got ignored or forgotten.

But cancer didn't go away just because you ignored it.

It still burned in him now, the memory of his parents' life together. It was a dull, red fire that he purposely kept smouldering—but not because he was waiting for the right woman to come along and rekindle it. His jaw clenched. No, it was there as a reminder of what happened when you let someone become your whole world and then you lost them and your whole world crumbled.

And that was another difference between him and Frankie.

She was still a believer—still looking to replace like with like, still hoping for something, or someone, to fill the gap in her life.

That someone wouldn't—couldn't—be him. What had happened with Harriet had only happened because he, like Frankie, had been young and alone and lost in grief. Yes, he had loved Harriet, but in a couple of months he would have probably loved someone else. And then someone else.

Only his life had just imploded, and his feelings for her had got mixed up with all the loss and the loneliness, and ultimately everything had been a disaster.

But it hadn't been without purpose. At least he could make sure that Frankie didn't make the same mistake.

He looked down at her hands, turning them over. They were so small and soft. *She* was soft—

he knew that now. Too soft for a world where you didn't need to be in Antarctica for life to be randomly brutal and harsh. Too soft to be in that world alone.

And one day she would find someone…someone special.

Blocking out the nip of jealousy at the thought of the faceless, nameless man who would one day hold Frankie close, he tightened his hand around hers.

For now, she just needed support.

'I find it helps to live in the moment,' he said slowly. 'To focus on the real and the present.'

Her eyes found his. 'Is that why you like sailing so much?'

He considered her question. 'I've never looked at it that way, but maybe yes.' Lifting her hand to his mouth, he kissed it gently. *'In vino veritas.'*

She grimaced. 'I haven't drunk that much.' Reaching for the bottle, she giggled. 'Oops… Perhaps I have. I don't normally like wine, but this is so delicious. All your wines are.'

He laughed then—not just at the wonder in her voice but at his own sudden and startling joy in the 'real and present' moment he was living. A moment he could enjoy in good faith, knowing that he was back in control.

'My father would have been deeply gratified to hear you say so. Wines were one of his three great loves.'

He saw the flicker of curiosity in her blue eyes—eyes that changed from moment to moment like the sea shimmering beneath the cliffs, so that first they were silver, then a dark indigo, and then the colour of amethysts.

'What were the other two?' she asked.

She had done it again. Resurrected the past so that he was thinking about his mother. Her face was clearer than Frankie's, the absence of her no less unthinkable and punitive now than it had been in those terrible first few days after her death.

He let a minute or two of silence tick by, but he could hardly ignore her question.

'That would be painting… And Helena. My mother,' he said slowly. 'Unfortunately for my grandfather.'

Frankie frowned. 'Why unfortunately?'

'That's how my parents met. My grandfather hired Lucien to paint my mother's portrait for her twenty-first birthday—'

'And they fell in love!' She ended his sentence triumphantly, excitement lighting up her face.

He nodded. 'Correct. And then they eloped. Over the border to Scotland. They planned it all in secret for months. Nobody knew anything about it until they called from Gretna Green.'

Frankie's eyes were wide and soft. 'That's so romantic.'

Leaning back, he studied the play of expressions on her face. Her excitement made him feel old and jaded. But that was a good thing. It meant he was back in control. It meant that moment earlier, when it had felt as if he was losing his footing, had been just a momentary lapse.

Holding her gaze, he shook his head. 'My grand-parents didn't think so. They were furious. Under-standably. Helena was only twenty, and Lucien was hardly ideal husband material.'

'He was a famous artist,' she protested.

'A forty-five-year-old artist with two failed mar-riages under his belt. And he wasn't that famous—not then. Plus, they'd already lined up a far more suitable husband-to-be. So, my uncles went and found her and brought her back home, kicking and screaming.'

She blinked. 'They did?'

He nodded, swept along by the familiar glam-our of the story despite himself. 'And then Lucien turned up at the house with a shotgun, threatening to shoot my grandfather, and got himself arrested.'

'Then what happened?'

The dazzle of eagerness in her eyes caught him like a punch to the solar plexus and he shrugged. 'Me. I happened.' He paused, staring at her steadily. 'My mother was already pregnant by then, and my grandparents realised they were fighting a lost cause.'

Watching her expression turn hazy, he felt a rush of vertigo. He could see it in her eyes. She was falling in love with the story and it sliced something open inside him.

'It's like a real-life fairy tale,' she said slowly.

His chest tightened. Most fairy tales ended with a wedding, not death and despair.

'You think?' He couldn't stop the note of bitterness from creeping into his voice.

'Of course.' She frowned. 'What could be more romantic?'

Her softly worded question pulled at his senses and, glancing over at her face, he tensed. She wanted to believe in happy-ever-after. Like most people, the aftermath—what happened when the happy-ever-after ended—didn't interest her so much.

He shrugged again. 'I suppose that would depend on your definition of "romantic".'

There was a small beat of silence and then Frankie looked him straight in the eye. 'Love conquers all. Every time.'

Turning his head, he glanced away from the open blueness of her gaze. 'Then I'd have to disagree with you.'

Frankie stared at him in confusion, separately and vividly aware of both the pulsing tension in his jaw and the distance in his eyes. She'd been having such a wonderful day. And it wasn't just the excitement of sailing on a real boat or the picnic which had taken her completely by surprise, it was Arlo.

Maybe it had been the freedom of being out on the boat, or perhaps if had been her opening up about her family yesterday, but he had talked more about his life in the last half-hour than he had done over the previous four days.

And that had been the sweetest surprise of all.

Only now it felt as if he had retreated into himself again.

She bit her lip. 'I don't understand…' she said slowly. 'How can you tell me that story and not believe in love?'

He shook his head. 'I'm not saying that.' His grey eyes held hers briefly, then flicked away again. 'My parents' love was mesmerising—like watching a magic trick. It was impossible to look away, not to be dazzled.'

She watched mutely as he stared up at the sky, his face expressionless.

'Their love was so intense and beautiful. It flooded the world around them and the people around them, like me, with this incredible light. It was like standing next to the sun.'

His mouth made a brief curve, painful to watch.

'But at the end of the day the sun is just a big star. All stars collapse, and when they do, they pull everything into the darkness with them.'

Frankie swallowed. She knew all about the darkness. The terrifying plummet into the abyss. But even though she knew that he'd lost both his parents, she hadn't thought that Arlo felt that. He seemed so in control, so invincible.

But what did she really know about his life... his past?

She hesitated, and then she took his hand and held it, feeling his tension against her thumb. 'How old were you when she died?'

He didn't reply, and for a moment she thought he wasn't going to, but then he said stiffly, 'Thirteen. I'd just started my first term at Eton. I didn't go back. I couldn't. Lucien was in such a state and Johnny was only two years old.'

Which was why Arlo hadn't ever been a prefect, she thought, her heart contracting.

'Didn't anyone help?' she asked.

'Lots of people tried. Family, friends... And the staff were all fantastic.' He sounded tired. Almost as if he was back in that huge, grief-filled house. 'But my father didn't want help. He wanted her. And when he realised he could never have her back he stopped crying and started raging against the world.'

Frankie shivered. He spoke as he wrote, each word chosen with a measured precision that only added pathos to his story.

'What did he do?'

Arlo's expression was bleak. 'He drank a lot. Smashed up his studio. Burned his paintings. Not all of them. Constance rescued some. Then he just gave up. He stayed in his pyjamas...he barely ate.'

'But who looked after you and Johnny?' Her voice sounded brittle—accusatory, even—but she didn't care. All she could think about was Arlo, all alone in the Hall with a tiny brother and a raging, unhappy man.

'Nannies on and off, at the beginning. They loved Johnny, but my father terrified them, so they never stayed long. Constance helped a lot. Mostly Johnny wanted me, and in the end we just muddled through.'

Her heart felt too big for her chest. Johnny had told her that Arlo had raised him, but she hadn't really believed him. 'What about you?' she whispered.

He shrugged. 'I didn't need looking after.' His beautiful, misshapen mouth twisted. 'And I wasn't easy to look after. Not like Johnny.'

Frankie nodded. She could all too easily imagine the awkward, brooding teenage Arlo, silent and trapped in his grief. Of course any nanny would prefer a beautiful, uncomplicated child like Johnny. She gritted her teeth, pushing back against the pressing weight of misery rising in her throat. Why did the world have to be so cruel? So unfair?

'I'm sorry,' she said quietly. 'I'm so sorry there was no one there for you.'

His face tensed. 'No, that's not how it was, Frankie. My uncles and aunts were fantastic. They sorted out all the financial stuff and the running of the Hall. But I wouldn't let them help with Lucien or Johnny.'

He looked up at her, his mouth twisting into a smile that made her hand tighten around his.

'As you know, I can be pretty stubborn when I want to be.'

'Why wouldn't you let them help?' she whispered.

For a moment he seemed lost in thought, and then his smile twisted tighter. 'I suppose I was trying to make amends.'

His voice was flat, dull, as if all the emotion had been ironed out of it.

She stared at him numbly. 'I don't understand...' Why would he need to make amends?

His eyes found hers, hearing the question even though she hadn't asked it.

'I knew she was ill. We all did. But my parents lived in this fantasy world of love and beauty and art. They ignored anything that was too "real". And I didn't want to face the truth on my own, so I let myself be persuaded to do nothing as well.'

The emptiness in his voice made the afternoon feel suddenly cool.

'I wanted to believe that their love could conquer everything, even though I knew unquestionably that it couldn't—that it was just a beautiful story.' He glanced over to where *The Aeolus* swayed against the tide. 'I made a choice, and it was the wrong one. I let my feelings override the facts.

After the funeral, I made a promise never to do that again.'

And he had kept his promise.

'So that's why you became a scientist. And why you don't believe in love.'

For some reason it hurt, saying those words out loud. Hurt more than it should. Almost more than knowing he'd been so lost and alone.

His eyes found hers, the clear sunlight touching the grey with silver. 'I didn't for a long time. But I do now.'

She couldn't speak. Suddenly her whole body was taut like a bowstring, and even though there was no reason to do so she was holding her breath. The beat of her heart hovered like a diver on the top board as she waited for his next sentence.

'For other people. Not for me. I could have done something—*should* have done something...told someone—but I didn't. I was like a child, watching the fireworks while the house burns down. And I know you're going to say I *was* just a child, but—'

'You were,' she said hoarsely, watching the tension in the tiny muscles around his mouth.

His jaw was taut, his eyes distant. 'I don't expect you to understand.'

But she did. She understood completely.

Love had let him down, failed him. No wonder he had turned his back on the world and chosen to spend his life wandering the icy extremities of the Arctic and Antarctica, putting his trust in science and data and brutal, honest facts.

It all made horrible, painful sense.

He had failed to save his mother so now he was trying to save the world. She understood that feeling. She felt the same the way—felt the same need to do penance and the urge to share that common chord—and her guilt was almost irresistible—

Her chest tightened. *Who was she trying to kid?* Nothing about her self-interested behaviour that night in France had anything to with the way Arlo had acted. And she wasn't about to burden him with her guilt.

Reaching up, she stroked his cheek. If she closed her eyes she could barely feel the scar. But scars were like icebergs: the damage ran deep.

'I do understand,' she said slowly.

If only that understanding came with some unique power to help his invisible scars heal, but she had nothing to offer him.

After they'd climbed back aboard *The Aeolus* Arlo turned towards the deck, but Frankie tightened her grip on his hand.

He frowned. 'I was just going to check in with the crew. Make sure everyone's okay.'

'They can manage without you.'

His eyes fixed on her face. 'Is this a mutiny?'

'Yes, it is,' she said softly and, feeling as if her

heart was dropping away from her body, she pulled him to her and kissed him softly.

She had been wrong. There *was* something that would soothe the pain. His and hers. Something that was in her power to give.

'You took care of me yesterday.' Her eyes locked with his and he breathed in sharply as she slid her hand between his thighs. 'Now it's my turn to take care of you.'

And, turning, she led him away from the deck and down to their cabin.

CHAPTER EIGHT

ROLLING ONTO HIS SIDE, Arlo stared across the room at the open bathroom door. Frankie was in the shower, and over the sound of the running water he could hear her singing. He couldn't make out the words of the song, but people only sang in the shower when they were happy and that was what mattered.

His shoulders tensed. Although after his performance yesterday she might be forgiven for not believing that.

Gazing unseeingly across the room, he thought about the things that he'd told Frankie out in the heather on the cliffs.

It shouldn't have happened. Ordinarily it wouldn't have. She was by no means the first woman to ask him about his parents, and he'd never had any trouble deflecting questions. But yesterday he hadn't been able to stop himself talking. And not just talking. It had been practically a full-blown confession. He had talked about everything.

Except Harriet.

But why would he mention his ex-wife?

It all seemed so long ago now.

He'd met her at university, just weeks after losing his father, when he had been desperate with grief. It shamed him to admit it now, but she had been a shoulder to cry on.

Except, of course, he hadn't cried.

Maybe if he had he might not have married her.

But he'd been young, and the impulsive flamboyance of marrying someone he barely knew had seemed like both the right way to honour his parents' love and a chance to give Johnny some kind of normality and stability.

But his marriage had been over before it had started, its only purpose seemingly to confirm what he'd already known. That love required a blind, unquestioning faith he'd lost.

His stomach tensed. Maybe it was no bad thing to remind himself of that—especially after last night. He wasn't made of stone or ice. Even if they hadn't been sleeping together, he cared about Frankie, and her story had broken his heart.

Not that there was any *real* risk to his heart. This was only about sex. Anything else was just a completely understandable impulse to look after someone who needed help.

He stared at the indentation in the pillow, where Frankie's head had been. Last night, after she'd fallen asleep, he'd looked up her family's accident on the internet, and the photos he'd found had left him feeling nauseous. There had been wreckage everywhere. A wing had been torn off and the plane looked as if it had been twisted like a wet cloth.

His chest tightened. Those pictures would stay with him for a long time. But not as long as that look on her face when she'd told him about the crash.

She had seemed so small and young and lost.

A dull ache spread out slowly inside him like spilt wine. He knew how that felt. Even now he could still remember it: the months spent watching his mother shrink in on herself, and then the years after her death, when his father had stopped being the huge, exuberant bear-like man of his childhood and became instead a child…a lonely, angry child who locked himself away with his pain.

But he was lucky. He'd had Johnny, and his family had always been there when he'd let them.

Speaking of family…

He shifted up the bed and, opening his bedside cabinet, pulled out an envelope. Inside was an invitation to his cousin Davey's tenth wedding anniversary party. And a request for him to say a few words.

He wasn't planning on going. He'd already hinted as much, pleading work, and by rights he wouldn't have even been in England if there hadn't been that problem with the plane, so…

He felt a stab of guilt. Davey wouldn't make a fuss about it, but he knew his cousin would be disappointed. But not surprised. And that made him feel even more guilty. Not that he was going to do anything about it. Much as he loved his family, he didn't do the big family events. They were just so full of an energy and emotion he couldn't handle.

Davey would understand. He'd call him and let him know…

The shower had stopped and, tossing the invitation to the top of the cabinet, he rolled on his back as Frankie wandered into the bedroom and instantly he forgot all about his cousin and the party.

Her hair was tied into some kind of bun thing, and she had a towel tied over her breasts so that her shoulders were bare. Staring over at her pale, damp skin, he felt his fingers itch to tug the towel loose.

'Nice shower?' he said softly.

She nodded. 'The best. Honestly, the water here is amazing. It's so hot and it's literally never-ending.'

Smiling, he reached for her hand and pulled her towards the bed. 'We use hydropower.'

'You mean like waves?'

'Sort of,' he said, pulling her onto his lap. 'There are caves under the island. When the sea floods them, we use three Archimedes screws to capture the energy of the flow, like a kind of reverse positive displacement… What? What is it?'

Frankie was staring at him, her expression soft, almost hazy.

'Nothing. I just—'

She steadied herself against his shoulders and he felt his body harden as her fingers splayed over his skin.

'Is there anything you don't know?' she asked.

Lots of things, he thought. *Like how she could look so beautiful with shadows under her eyes.*

Or how she had walked away from that crash alive.

Pushing that thought away, he looked into her eyes. 'Plenty, but if the subject interests me enough I make it my business to find out everything there is to know.'

I see.' She shifted against him in a way that made his hands clamp around her waist. 'So what kind of subjects currently interest you?'

'Well, just lately I've grown very interested in social media.'

He watched as she let her hair down, shaking it loose so that it tumbled over her shoulders.

'Anything else?'

'Billiards.'

'Really?'

This time as she shifted the towel flared around her hips and a tingle of heat tightened his muscles as he caught a glimpse of red-gold curls.

'Anything else?' she asked again, softly.

'Foxes.' He sucked in a breath as she leaned forward and ran a finger down the dark line of hair bisecting his abdomen. 'Female foxes in particular.'

The small smile tugging at the corners of her

mouth made a complex mix of heat and tension spike inside him.

'And how do you plan on finding out about female foxes?' she asked.

He cleared his throat. 'I'll start with a thorough and exhaustive examination of any previous research.' As her hand slid beneath the bedclothes, his hands tightened around the edges of the towel. 'Although I'm guessing that sounds a little academic and dry.'

'Maybe a little academic...' Raising her hips, she tugged the towel loose and let it fall down her body. Their eyes met and he moved his hands up her back, caressing the indentation of her waist as she lifted her hips and then lowered herself onto him. 'But definitely not dry.'

He sucked in a sharp breath. She was warm, slick, tight. 'That's good,' he said through gritted teeth. 'That's so good.'

'Then what will you do?' she whispered.

She was shivering as if she was cold, but her skin felt hot and smooth, like sun-baked sand.

'I'll go out into the field...do some hands-on research of my own.'

He cupped her breasts, his thumbs grazing her nipples so that she arched forward, her mouth forming a long, slow amorphous syllable. He felt his control snap. Reaching up, he brought her face down to his and kissed her fiercely, his groan of pleasure mingling with hers as he rolled her beneath him and surrendered to the impossible need building inside them.

Later, tucked against his warm body, Frankie lay with her head against Arlo's chest, listening to his heartbeat.

She was still trying to catch her breath.

Each time it happened she kept expecting it to be different. For the spell to be broken, the magic to have gone. But each time was the same.

Not the same, she corrected herself. That made it sound boring, and in bed, as in life, Arlo was adventurous and passionate and tireless.

He felt so good. Big and warm and strong, so that even in the eye of the storm, when his hard body was driving into hers, she could sense the solid core of him. And afterwards, in his arms, she felt so calm, so safe.

Closing her eyes, she turned her face into the hollow beneath his shoulder, breathing in his scent. She could feel body softening against his. Except it wasn't just her body that was softening. The last few days had turned everything she'd thought to be true on its head, so that it was hard to believe she had once found him horrible and rude and arrogant.

And it wasn't just the sex. Yesterday, he had been kind to her, and gentle—tender, almost—and it was making her feel tender towards him. Particularly after what he'd told her about his parents.

And it was okay to feel that way, she thought defensively. There was no need to overthink it. It wasn't as if she was in love with him or anything.

'What are you thinking?'

She blinked. Arlo was looking down at her, his eyes resting on her face. Hoping very much that he couldn't read her thoughts, she said quickly, 'Just about how beautiful it looks outside.'

His hand touched her hip bone and he ran his finger lightly along the curve of her bottom. 'Not as beautiful as you.'

Her eyes met his. 'So, do you have anything planned for today?' She wriggled away from his hand, laughing. 'Aside from *that*.'

'No, nothing. I'm entirely at your disposal.'

She breathed out shakily. In one way it was a relief to feel that stab of hunger, to be reminded that this was all about sex. But it was starting to scare her how much she needed him.

And it *was* a need. A requirement like air or water.

She couldn't imagine life without him. Only at some point she was not only going to have to imagine it, but experience it for real.

She couldn't stay here for ever. Her life was in London and that wasn't going to change, however good the sex or however momentarily kind Arlo was, and there was no point in imagining anything more permanent.

'Let me see what time it is,' she said, needing

to move away from the heat of his body, or at least to prove that she could.

Leaning past him, she grabbed his watch.

'Oh, sorry.' She reached down for the card that she'd knocked to the floor. Unthinkingly, she glanced at it. It was an invitation to a wedding anniversary party.

'Who's Davey and Serena?'

'My cousin and his wife. It's their tenth wedding anniversary.'

Arlo's voice was clipped and, glancing up, she saw that the easy intimacy of moments earlier had faded. Now he looked guarded, wary.

'That's wonderful. And they're having a party.' She gave him a small stiff smile. 'Don't worry— I'm not angling for a plus-one. I'll be long gone by—' She broke off, her eyes widening as she read the date. 'But it's today.' Looking up, she frowned. 'I don't understand. Why didn't you say something?'

'Why would I? I'm not attending.'

Even without the sudden coolness in his voice she would have sensed that as far as Arlo was concerned this particular topic of conversation was over.

'But why? It's a special occasion.' Her stomach clenched. 'It's not anything to do with me, is it?'

He frowned. 'I'm sorry to break this to you, Frankie, but very little in my life is anything to do with you.' His eyes were hard now. 'We're not over-thinking this. That's what we agreed, remember?'

Frankie stared at him, mute with shock, feeling a chill slide over her skin at the starkness of his words. 'I remember.'

'Good.' He rolled off the bed and stalked past her naked. 'And, just so we're clear, I'm not going to be running my social diary past you any time soon.'

'I'm not expecting you to. I just thought it had to be me…the reason you aren't going. I mean, what other reason could there be?' she persisted. 'It's not as if you're doing anything else…and it's your cousin's anniversary party.'

Pulling on his trousers, he shook his head. 'My reasons are my business, and this conversation is over.'

She held her breath, hanging on to her temper. 'Why are you being like this? I was just trying to be nice.' Turning, fists clenching, she took a step towards him. 'What is the matter? I don't under-stand—'

'Then let me make it plain.' There was no emotion in his voice. 'What I do, where I go or don't go, is nothing to do with you. And that goes for my family too.'

She stared at him, her anger fading, giving way to a savage, wrenching pain that made tears choke up in her throat.

'You're right. It isn't my business. Nor is it my

family. I think I just forgot that for a moment.' She balled her hands, trying to contain all the chaos and emotion inside her. 'I was thinking about *my* family and how I'd give anything just to see them again—'

The room swam.

'Frankie—'

She held up a defensive hand. 'It's fine. I don't need you to comfort me. I can deal with it on my own.'

'Please— Please!' He took a step closer. 'Please don't cry. I never want to make you cry.'

Her eyes burned as he caught her, his hands gripping her shoulders.

'I'm sorry,' he said. 'I didn't mean what I said. I don't know why I said it. It's not even true, and now I've upset you—'

She breathed out shakily. His misery was palpable—as was his remorse. 'Not everything is about you, Arlo. I'm upset because I lost my family. And, yes, you made me think about them. But I've spent the last two years not being able to do that, so that's a *good* thing.'

And it was true. She didn't feel trapped or alone with her loss anymore; in fact, she actually felt more, not less, in control.

'I don't mind getting upset, but I do mind you talking to me like that. I don't deserve that—'

'No, you don't.' He pulled her against him, his

thumbs tightening around her wrists. 'I'm sorry,' he said again.

The features of his face were so familiar, but his expression wasn't. He looked troubled, young, unsure of himself.

'It's just the idea of a party... I'm not like you. I'm not a people person.'

Wasn't he? She stared at him in confusion. Arlo seemed to have good relationships with everyone at the Hall, and Johnny adored him.

'But they're your *family*.'

He nodded. 'Yes, and I love them. It's just being with all of them all together is hard for me.' He hesitated. 'But you're right. It's a special occasion. I should be there. I *need* to be there.' Looking down at her, he clasped her face, stroking her hair. 'And I'd like you to be there with me.'

Her heart bumped. 'Arlo, you don't need to... That wasn't why—'

'I know it wasn't. And I don't need you there— I want you there.'

'Are you being serious?'

He nodded slowly. 'Of course.' His hand found hers. 'Please, Frankie. I really do want you to come with me. Davey's home, Stanhope Park, is an amazing place. There's a pool, and horses, and Davey's organised a clay pigeon shoot for the morning after.'

She bit her lip. 'It all sounds lovely, but I don't have anything to wear to a party.'

'Wear what you wore the other night,' he said softly. 'I promise not to strip it off you this time.'

Their eyes met and her fingers twitched as his words sent a current of heat from his hand to hers, so that she was suddenly vibrating inside.

Why not go? It would be fun to dress up and dance. And, despite having recovered his composure, Arlo clearly found this kind of event hard. Her eyes snagged on a puckered scar on his chest. He had helped her so much…maybe it was time for her to help him.

She screwed up her face. 'You're sure your cousin won't mind? Me just turning up?'

'I'll call him, but he won't mind. Davey's not like that. He's a good man. Kind. Loyal. A little bit cautious.' He smiled one of those almost-smiles that made her world tilt off its axis. 'But then he's spent years being the son and heir.'

She pinched her lip, feeling suddenly nervous. 'So what do I call him?'

'His full title is Viscount Fairfax, but in person he's just Davey.' He rubbed at the worry lines between her eyebrows. 'Look…straight up, the house is a bit full-on. But they're very normal people who do very normal things, like have lunch with their family.'

Frankie nodded. It would be all right. In London she met all kinds of people all the time for her work. But then she hadn't ever cared what they thought. Arlo was different. She didn't want to let him down.

She didn't want to let her own family down either.

A knot was forming in her stomach. That *she* should have survived was the cruellest cut of all. So many times she had wondered why she alone had been spared, and she was still no closer to knowing the answer... All she knew was that she had to make her life count and make them proud.

His dark gaze roamed her face. 'You don't believe me?'

Glancing up, she tried to smile, tried to hide the conflicting emotions swirling inside her.

'I do. I just don't want to mess up,' she said slowly.

'I wouldn't worry about that.'

'But you're not me,' she said slowly. 'You don't have anything to prove.'

He hesitated, and she wondered if, like her, he was hearing an echo of that moment out on the hillside above the Hall. Only that had been teasing, rhetorical... They both knew Arlo had nothing to prove. Whereas she...

'Everyone has something to prove,' Arlo said quietly. 'Look at Davey. He owns a twenty-thousand-acre estate, but he didn't earn the money to buy it.' His hand touched her cheek. 'He inherited it from his father, along with his title. That was the easy part. Now he has to run it well enough so that it will be there for *his* son to inherit. He wants to do the best he can.'

'I want that too.' She could hear the emotion in her voice but didn't try to stop it. 'After the accident, I made a promise I'd do everything I could to make my family proud of me.'

'I'm sure they were proud, Frankie...' Frowning, he tried to cup her chin.

But, batting his hand away, she shook her head. 'Proud of what? The fact that I spent all my time on my phone? Messed up my exams? Dropped out of university? It's not exactly most parents' outcome of choice for their child.'

'Did they say that?'

She made herself look at him. He was watching her calmly. 'Of course not. They weren't like that. They weren't like me.'

They were like Arlo. High achievers. Top of everything they tried.

'My dad was a paediatrician. My mum was a barrister. Harry was a junior doctor and Amelie was a solicitor. But they weren't trophy-hunters they were good people...'

Better than good. They'd been decent, dependable, far more deserving of life.

Suddenly she was unbearably conscious of her guilt.

His brows drew together. '*You're* a good person, Frankie. And I don't believe for one moment that your family would want you thinking like this.'

The vehemence in his voice made her breath catch in her throat, but it was his hands, with their firm, unwavering grip, that steadied her. She felt a lightness inside her that seemed momentarily to reframe the choices she'd made.

He didn't have to do this, she thought. Take time to reassure her. Leaning forward, she kissed his cheek, her lips soft and warm against his skin. 'You're a good person too,' she said slowly.

As he let his head rest against hers she felt her heart contract. Since losing her family, the idea of getting close to someone, caring about them, had been too terrifying to contemplate. She couldn't risk it happening again. To love and then lose someone again was beyond her. That was why she kept people at arm's length, built emotional barriers between herself and the world.

Until Arlo. Seeing him so vulnerable had made something crack open inside her. But she had to keep things straight in her head. Maybe one day she would be able to love and be loved, but not here, not now, not with him.

This could only ever be temporary, and these feelings of tenderness were just the result of her loneliness and her desire to belong somewhere.

And besides, Arlo didn't even believe in love.

He let his head rest against hers. 'You'll have fun, okay? I promise. Now, get dressed and pack whatever you think you'll need. I've just got a couple of calls to make.'

* * *

'I got Robert to bring the car round,' Arlo said, turning to Frankie as they walked downstairs. 'But I thought I'd drive myself.'

Glancing discreetly at his watch, he felt a ripple of astonishment as he saw the time. Incredibly, it had taken an hour and a half for Frankie to pack, but he'd waited patiently, sensing that to rush her would be counterproductive.

She had been nervous before, but now she seemed excited and he was the one feeling jittery.

No, not jittery so much as conflicted.

He wanted to go, for Frankie's sake, but he was still dreading it. Partly that was because he'd never been as extroverted as Johnny and his parents, and he found spending time with his family *en masse* hard. But mostly the reason he didn't want to go was because celebrating Davey and Serena's tenth anniversary would remind him of his own failed marriage.

His stomach clenched. It was so unbelievably petty and shameful that he could barely admit it to himself, much less Frankie. Only she'd said that thing about her own family and he'd had to pull himself together.

She shook her head. 'I still can't believe I know someone who has a chauffeur.'

He shrugged. 'It's not that big a deal. It's just a useful option if I need to take my hands off the wheel.'

Watching her bite into her lip, he felt his insides clench.

'You have a one-track mind,' he said softly.

Her blue eyes locked with his, wide and teasing. 'So do you.'

'You carry on looking at me like that and I'm going to have to put you in the boot,' he warned.

She laughed. 'Empty threats, Milburn. The Land Rover doesn't have a boot.'

'We're not going in the Land Rover, Fox,' he said, holding open the front door.

Turning, she clamped her hand to her mouth. 'Oh, my goodness. Is that a Rolls-Royce?'

The note of excitement in her voice was strangely satisfying, and he let his gaze follow hers to where the huge golden convertible crouched like a lion in the drive.

'So this is the car Robert drives.' She giggled. 'I couldn't imagine you being driven around in state in your Land Rover. But this makes more sense.'

Reaching out, she slid her fingers over the silver figurine crouching on the bonnet and he felt almost light-headed. It was dizzyingly easy to imagine those same small, delicate hands caressing his body.

'Does she have a name?' she asked.

'She does.' He cleared his throat. 'The Spirit of Ecstasy.'

Her eyes met his, a small smile tugging at the corners of her mouth. 'I'll bear that in mind.'

* * *

'Are we here?' Only a little while later, Frankie was glancing out of her window. Up ahead, a pair of huge wrought-iron gates rose up between the high brick walls edging the road.

He nodded. 'This is it. Stanhope Park.' Leaning over, he punched a number into the keypad set into the wall and waited as the gates swung open.

As the big car swept up the driveway Frankie suddenly sat up straighter, her cheeks flushed with excitement and awe. 'Oh, wow,' she said five minutes later, as he pulled up in front of the beautiful house.

Switching the engine off, he looked over at her. 'Okay?'

'Yes.' She nodded, and then she froze, her blue eyes widening with panic. 'But what have you told them? About *us*?' She stumbled over the word. 'I mean, about who I am...what I am to you?'

He stared at her in silence, his heart beating against his ribs, stunned by her question and by his own idiocy. It was the first question everyone would ask, only up until now he hadn't thought to classify their relationship. It hadn't seemed necessary. In fact, naming what he and Frankie shared felt wrong, for some reason.

But this was going to be hard enough as it was. He didn't need to complicate matters by questioning what was, in essence, just a fling. He should follow his own advice and not overthink things.

'I think it'll make things simpler if we stick as close to the truth as possible. Why don't we just say we met through Johnny and you're up from London for a couple of days?'

She didn't say anything for a moment, and then she nodded slowly. 'That would work.'

'Good,' he said brusquely as the front door opened and a trio of Labradors came cantering out, followed by a tall blond man. 'Now, come and meet Davey.'

Arlo had been right about his cousin, she thought, as Davey led them into the house. He seemed like a really nice, normal man. But, despite what Arlo had said earlier, it was difficult not to be intimidated by Stanhope Park.

It was as big as a hotel, and if it hadn't been for the fact that Davey was wearing a Tattersall check shirt, moleskin jeans, and tan-coloured brogues she would have felt as if she'd slipped through a looking glass into the seventeenth century.

Lavish gilding, Rococo tapestries and jewel-bright festoon curtains were perfectly offset by a neutral colour palette of French grey, buff, and pale green. In fact, everything was perfect, she thought, gazing round their vast bedroom.

'I'll leave you to get settled in.' Davey smiled at Frankie. 'Lunch is at two.'

Lunch. She walked slowly the length of the room, trailing her fingers over the smooth velvet and polished wood, then walked back to where Arlo was watching her calmly.

'So...?' He tilted his head back questioningly.

'It's a little intimidating.' She met his gaze. 'Should I change for lunch?' She looked down at her jeans and sweater.

He shook his head. 'But, speaking of clothes, I have something for you.' Taking her hand, he led her past the gloriously over the top canopied bed and into the dressing room. 'I hope you like it.'

Frankie stared past him, open-mouthed, at a curaçao-blue silk dress. Except that dress was too basic a word for the confection hanging from the rail. Thin, fragile straps, a flowing skirt... Turning the dress, she felt her pulse accelerate. And a devastating neckline cut low to reveal the length of her back.

'Where...? How did you...?' she stammered.

'Bond Street. I had them courier it up.' His eyes were fixed on her face, examining her reaction. 'I took a punt at your measurements, so I hope it fits.'

'Oh, Arlo.' She breathed out shakily. 'It's lovely...but I can't accept this.'

'Of course you can. I invited you, remember? And after I spoke to Serena I realised the party was going to be bigger and grander than I thought.'

'Grander!' Her head was spinning. 'You mean, like crowns and things?'

Shaking his head, he brushed her hair back around her ear. 'No, it's just that the guest list is a bit of a roll-call of the great and the good. They like to dress up and I want you to feel at home.'

There was no dress on earth that could do that, she thought dully.

'Who are they?' she heard herself say.

'There's my other cousins, Jack and Arthur. Jack runs a very successful hedge fund and his wife Charlotte co-owns an art gallery in Knightsbridge. Arthur owns an estate over the border in Scotland, and his wife Jemma is a model. Then there's Tom—he set up a literacy charity...'

She felt hot and shivery, as if she had a fever. Maybe she did have one. It would certainly explain why she wasn't thinking straight...why she had agreed to this. What had she been thinking? It was hard enough to pretend to herself that she was good enough. She couldn't possibly spend an evening trying to convince people like Arlo's friends and family.

'I'm sorry, I don't think I can do this.'

'Do what?' Arlo looked straight into her eyes. He sounded confused.

'Be here. In this house. With these people.' Her hands were tingling now, and she felt a rush of panic, cold and swirling and unstoppable, like the waves rising up over the causeway. 'I thought I could, but I don't fit in here. I don't own an estate. I'm not a lady.'

'So what? I'm not a lord...' The confusion in his eyes had darkened his irises almost to black.

'But you're related to one. And you own an island.' Her heart was crashing in her ears. 'You've walked to the South Pole alone. Everyone at this party will have done something amazing, won't they?'

'And so have you.' His hands caught her wrists. 'Look, Frankie, I get that you're still grieving, but you have got to stop this. You've got to let go.'

Her heart squeezed. 'Of what?'

'This need you feel to be worthy of life.' He was looking at her, his face implacable. 'Look, I understand. You see it all the time in the military. Survivor's guilt. A belief that you did something wrong by surviving. That being alive makes you guilty.'

In a tiny voice, she said, 'But I *am* guilty.'

'Of what? Surviving something that was completely random?'

'Not just surviving.' She drew a breath, trying to maintain control. 'It's my fault they're dead.'

Heart hammering, Arlo stared at her in silence. Her voice sounded as if it was sticking in her throat. She looked frightened, angry, *helpless*.

It was like seeing himself at thirteen.

Pushing that thought away, he shook his head. 'It wasn't your fault, Frankie. It was an accident.'

She pulled away from him, her anger rearing up like a riderless horse. 'How would you know? You weren't there?'

'No, I wasn't,' he agreed. 'But there was an inquest. People must have looked into what happened—'

'Other people who weren't there either.' The skin was taut across her cheekbones. 'They don't know what happened. What I did.' Her face contracted.

'Then tell me.' He looked at her, waiting. 'Tell me what you did.'

The anger that had flared up so fiercely flickered and died. 'I made my dad fly that night. He was tired, and he said it was too late, but I made a huge fuss about getting home because I wanted to go to some stupid party. I knew he didn't want to fly, but I made him—'

The despair in her eyes made his skin sting. This was more than just grief, and the crash had robbed her of more than just her family. It had taken away her trust. Not just that childlike faith shared by everyone that nothing bad could happen to good people, but faith in herself, in the person she'd thought she was.

Shaking his head, he kept his voice gentle but firm. 'Your dad was the pilot, Frankie. And he decided to fly. It was his decision. Not your mum's. Not yours. His.'

'So what are you saying? That it was *his* fault?'

The anger was back and he caught her wrists again.

'It was nobody's fault. Including yours. But you

want it to be. Because your guilt is a way of holding on to the people you've lost.' She stared up at him mutely and, loosening his grip, he reached up and stroked her cheek. 'Or you think it is. But you end up losing them anyway, because you can't bear thinking about them, talking about them.'

She took a small shuddering breath and, watching her press her hand against her mouth, he felt his throat constrict. But he carried on relentlessly.

'And I know that's not what you want. But if you want to remember them you have to accept that what happened wasn't some sort of cosmic *quid pro quo*. They didn't die so you could live. You have to accept that and forgive yourself for not dying.'

Her small, white upturned face was like one of the anemones that grew beneath the walls of his kitchen garden.

'I don't know how,' she whispered.

'But I do, sweetheart. Trust me.' His fingers tightened around hers. 'You do trust me, don't you, Frankie?'

'Yes,' she whispered. 'I do.'

'Then you've taken the first step.'

Her face dissolved into tears and, wordlessly, Arlo pulled her against his body, his own eyes burning, his whole being focused on the aim of making the infinite expanse of her grief measurable.

Stroking her hair, he talked soothingly, and finally she breathed out shakily.

'I'm sorry. I always seem to be crying all over you.'

'You need to cry.' Lifting her chin, he kissed her softly on the lips. 'And I have plenty of shirts.'

She folded her body against his trustingly and he tensed inside. He had asked her to trust him, but why? He didn't want her trust. He didn't need that burden. He knew he should move, only his hand kept caressing her hair, and he could feel her soft warmth taking him to a place where cynicism and loneliness didn't play any part.

But even if that place existed it was not for him, and he lifted his hand as she tilted her head back to look at him.

'You'd better go and change, then, before we go down to lunch,' she said, her fingers lightly touching the front of his shirt. 'I seem to have covered this one in mascara.'

'Are you sure you want to stay?'

The shaky smile that accompanied her nod was something he couldn't bear to look at, and he pulled her closer.

'You're not responsible for what happened. No one is. Life is cruel and random, but you're not alone. I meant what I said. I'm here.'

Not for ever, of course. But that was a given. They both knew what this was, and how it would end. And it *would* end…

CHAPTER NINE

TAKING A STEP back from the mirror, Frankie held a breath, her eyes meeting her reflection with silent satisfaction.

She'd kept her make-up simple—just smoky eyes, mascara, a pinkish lip tint—and her hair was pinned up with just a few loose curls framing her face. It was the dress…the beautiful blue dress… that was the star of the show.

It was a dress that managed to be revealing and subtle at the same time. A dress that made her look sleek, sophisticated, and wholly unfamiliar.

Turning, she glanced over her shoulder at the back of the dress. Her pulse jumped like a startled frog.

What back?

She was naked from the top of her spine right down to the twin indentations above the curve of her bottom, and yet she didn't feel exposed. In fact, she had worn far less revealing dresses and felt more vulnerable.

Breathing out shakily, she ran her hand over the smooth, shimmering silk. In part, that was down to how the dress hugged her body, almost protectively. The other reason—the main reason, of course—that she didn't feel vulnerable tonight was Arlo.

Her pulse twitched.

'Trust me,' he'd said, and then, 'You do trust me, don't you?'

And there had been no doubt, not even an atom of hesitation, in her reply. Her trust in him was as unwavering and unequivocal as the man himself. How could it not be? After everything he'd done and said.

Her throat tightened. After the inquest she had stopped talking to people about the accident, about the part she felt she'd played. Instead, she had kept her guilt close, preferring it to the alternative, more crushing pain of loss.

Only she could see now that hiding the truth had meant also hiding who she was, so she'd created Frankie Fox the social media influencer with a million friends—none of whom knew her, all of whom were easy to keep at arm's length.

But she hadn't kept Arlo at arm's length, and in his arms the truth had come pouring out. Today, though, he hadn't just listened. He had forced her to confront the whole truth, made her see that her guilt wasn't just trapping her but condemning her family to exist only in those few terrible, fractured moments.

He had made it possible for her to move past that terrible night in France and it had been like a weight lifting. The pain of losing them was still there, it always would be, but she could live with that now that the other terrible, relentless ache was gone.

Her head had been so fuzzy with adrenaline and emotion that she still didn't really know how he'd done it. But one fragment of memory was diamond-bright.

Arlo had rescued her. *Again.*

Not from a swirling sea, but from herself.

And she wanted to say something—only what? *Thank you* seemed too anodyne. But she didn't know how to express the complicated mix of emotions she was feeling. Maybe the right words would just come to her after a glass of champagne...

Wondering if Arlo was ready to go, she turned and headed back into the bedroom.

She stopped in the doorway, her heart skipping a beat.

He was slumped on the sofa, reading a book. His hair was still a little damp from the shower, but he was more than ready, in a dinner jacket that accentuated his broad shoulders, matching trousers, another snow-white shirt, and, finishing it off like a ribbon on a birthday present, a perfectly knotted bow tie.

Her stomach did a slow backwards flip.

If only she could spend the evening slowly unwrapping him.

But, taking a second look, she felt her breathing slow. Despite the casual arrangement of his limbs, there was something about how he was sitting…an almost unnatural stillness that hinted at the coiled tension beneath his skin.

Remembering his agitation earlier, she felt a fierce protective urge, cold and potent like a shot of vodka. He was on edge—not that he would admit it. He'd said all he'd wanted to earlier—probably more than he'd wanted, in fact. But she knew. And more importantly, she knew what to do about it. He had given her this beautiful dress, but she would take care of him tonight—that would be her gift to him.

As though sensing her scrutiny, Arlo looked up. Clearing her throat, she took a step forward and did a little twirl. 'How do I look?'

He got to his feet, his grey eyes sweeping admiringly over her body. 'Like a goddess,' he said softly.

He closed the distance between them in two strides and the iron strength of his arm anchored her against him as his lips found hers. Sliding her hands up over his satin lapels, she breathed out shakily against his mouth. Her body was softening…her skin was growing warm, too warm. In another few seconds the small amount of resolve she had would melt away…

'Arlo—'

He broke away. 'I know. I know…'

His smile was rigid as she reached up to wipe her lipstick from his mouth. 'That's better,' she said lightly. 'I'm just going to touch up my lips.' She was back in less than a minute. 'Okay, I'm ready.'

'Not quite.' He was holding out a slim black velvet box.

Her heart felt suddenly as though it was trying to beat a path through her ribs. 'What's that?' she croaked.

'Open it and see,' he said quietly.

Speechless with shock, she stared down at a beautiful diamond bracelet. 'You shouldn't have—' Her lower lip was quivering. 'No, I mean it. You've already given me this beautiful dress.'

'That was a necessity. So is this, actually.' Lifting the delicate band, he opened the clasp and slipped it onto her wrist. 'Don't you know, darling? It's the accessories that make the dress.'

That wasn't true, she thought, glancing down at the smooth blue silk. This dress had been perfect as it was. This was generous, thoughtful, *personal*.

She felt her heartbeat accelerate. Arlo had wanted to see her reaction, to make her happy. *But only because he did things properly*, she told herself firmly. And probably that was how he'd been raised. It wasn't personal.

'Arlo, you can't keep buying me things,' she protested.

'Why? It gives me pleasure.' He stared down

at her, his grey eyes intent and enveloping. 'You wouldn't want to stop giving me pleasure, would you?'

'No, but I don't have a gift for you…'

Her voice trailed off as he leaned forward and she felt his lips trace the pulse down her neck. The room blurred and a ribbon of heat uncurled inside her. Would it always be like this with him? So instant, so intense, so annihilating.

More importantly, could it ever be like this with another man?

Arlo lifted his head and the room slowly stopped spinning. 'We should probably go…'

His hand was warm and firm around hers. She smiled. 'Then let's go.'

Frankie could hear the party as soon as Arlo opened their bedroom door. Downstairs, guests were spilling out of the rooms, and it didn't take long for her to realise that not only did most of them know Arlo, many of them were surprised to see him.

Clearly he'd been telling the truth about not enjoying big family events.

He hid it well. His face was blank of expression, aside from the occasional stiff smile, but his arm was rigid beneath hers and she could feel his discomfort.

Only, somehow, knowing that he found it so difficult made it easier for her to step forward and smile and talk and laugh.

This was something she enjoyed—something she could do well, she realised. But, more than that, it was her chance to do something for him. Her chance to make him feel as safe and protected as he'd made her feel out on the causeway.

As they made their way to the ballroom Frankie caught her breath. In daylight, the house was astonishing. Now, though, it looked magical. Like an enchanted fairy tale palace.

Canopies of tiny lights hung down the walls behind huge displays of pink and cream roses, and beneath their feet an immaculate checkerboard marble floor gleamed beneath rows of glittering chandeliers.

The guests were pretty impressive too, she thought, her eyes leapfrogging over the men's immaculate monochrome evening wear to the sparkling dresses and plunging necklines of their wives and girlfriends.

Everyone looked so relaxed and happy.

Everyone but Arlo, she thought, her eyes darting to the man beside her and the lines of tension around his eyes.

'Here.' Plucking two glasses of champagne from the tray of a passing waiter, he handed her one.

'Thank you—oh, wow!'

Gazing up at the soaring ceiling, Frankie felt as if she'd already drunk the contents of her glass.

Arlo leaned into her, his body warm against the cool skin of her back. 'My great-great-great-great-grandfather is the one in the middle.'

'You mean the one kneeling in front of that woman wearing a sheet? I guess he does look a little like you from this angle,' she said softly.

Looking up at him, she was struck again by his size and his austere, uncompromising features, but most of all by his intense maleness. Other men might be prettier, more symmetrical, more elegant, but Arlo was magnificent. And half a head taller than everyone else.

She felt a slight fluttering pressure against her pelvic bone as he stared down at her, his eyes dark with heat. Taking a breath, she said quickly, 'So why did he get to be painted on the ceiling?'

Arlo glanced upward. 'He actually got more than a ceiling. This estate was a gift for his military successes against the French and the Bavarians.'

'And you followed in his footsteps?'

He met her eyes. 'Not quite. Although I did get into a fight with a French geologist out at Svalbard a couple of years back.'

'What happened?'

'He was uncomplimentary about my sledge.'

Frankie burst out laughing. Watching some of the tension leave his face, she felt her happiness grow brighter than the light from the polished chandeliers.

'Oh, there you are!'

It was Serena, glamorous in silver *lamé*, and the warmth in her voice matched her smile. Beside her, Davey was handsome in his dark suit.

'Davey was worried you'd got lost. He was about to send a search party.'

Arlo shook his cousin's hand. 'As if I'd miss the chance to razz you in public.' He turned to Serena and kissed her on the cheek. 'You look lovely as always, Lady Fairfax.'

'Never mind me.' Turning, she gazed admiringly at Frankie. 'Look at you. You look absolutely gorgeous. Doesn't she, Arlo?'

Frankie felt her blood lighten as his eyes rested on her face, his head tilting slightly towards her. 'Yes, she does.'

Frankie was more than gorgeous, Arlo thought, pressing his hand flat on her back to steady himself. She was captivatingly lovely. He literally couldn't tear his gaze away from her.

The *crème de ciel* blue silk not only matched her eyes, it seemed to ripple over her body like water, and he had to concentrate hard on keeping his hands from sliding aside those thin straps.

Later, he told himself firmly, as his cousin Arthur bounded up to greet him. Later in their room, when they were alone, he would strip her naked and take her in his arms and let his body flow into hers.

Right now, he had to get through this.

Although with Frankie by his side it was proving less painful than he'd anticipated. Her excitement was infectious and, standing beside her, he was struck by how easily she got on with people. She made it look so effortless. Considering she didn't know anyone, she was relaxed and natural and warm—in other words, everything he wasn't. And it was obvious that she accepted people for who they were.

Just as she had accepted him.

But he could see, too, that she loved being part of a family again—and she *was* a part of it. She fitted into his world like a hand in a glove.

As if sensing his gaze, Frankie glanced over at him and he felt his heartbeat accelerate. The skin was taut over the curves of her cheekbones, her eyes glittering with a curiosity and eagerness for life. *For him.*

His breath caught. When she looked at him like that it was tempting to think beyond the here and now, beyond this evening, beyond tomorrow...

Tempting, too, to think of choices made and yet to be made, of tantalising possibilities that had nothing to do with cold and danger or hardship and isolation, so that suddenly it was easy to imagine an alternative, hazy, sun-filled world, where the sky was always the colour of curaçao and Frankie was always in his bed.

But he'd chased that dream before, and all

he'd succeeded in doing was breaking Harriet's heart and proving to himself what he had already known. Feelings could not be relied upon.

So why go there? Why ruin what they had?

This was perfection. A flawless moment frozen in time. It was not for everyone, but for him it was the only way.

From across the room, he heard someone call his name. Glancing over, he saw Arthur holding up his wrist and pointing at his watch.

It was time. The moment he'd been dreading was finally upon him.

Right on cue, a waiter appeared by his side and, picking up the glass of champagne from the tray, Arlo tapped it imperiously with a spoon.

Instantly the conversations around him subsided into silence and, moving purposefully through the crowd, he made his way over to the stage that had been set up for the band.

'Thank you. Most of you already know me. But for those that don't my name is Arlo and Davey is my cousin. I know pretty much everything there is to know about him. But today isn't just about Davey. As you all know, today is Davey and Serena's tenth wedding anniversary.'

There was a small smattering of applause and a few cheers and he waited until they died away.

'And I was there, as most of you were, ten years ago, when they made their vows. Vows they have kept faithfully.' Turning towards his cousin and

Serena, he forced his mouth to soften into a smile. 'As we all knew they would. Their vows were the real deal. Made with love.'

A love he envied and feared in equal measure.

He cleared his throat. 'The kind of love that is an ever-fixed mark—that hasn't changed and won't change with the passing of time or be shaken by storms.'

As he looked out across the mass of faces his eyes connected with Frankie's and he felt as if his heart was dropping away from his body, remembering what he'd said about love to her.

'And that love is why we love them. Why we love spending time with them. Why we're all here tonight.'

The words tasted bitter on his tongue. Each one a reminder of how he'd failed in his own marriage—a marriage that had served only to prove that his parents' rapturous, unfettered joy in one another was beyond his reach.

Someone coughed and he returned his attention to his audience.

'To sum up: money might make the world go round, but Davey and Serena are proof that love is the coin of the realm. Their love for one another, for their beautiful son Bertie, and for all of us.' He raised his glass. 'And now we have a chance to honour that love. So please raise your glasses and join me in a toast to Davey and Serena. For making it all look so easy.'

Everyone chanted out the names and then there was a huge cheer. He felt a relief that was more intoxicating than any champagne flood his veins.

It was over.

'Thanks, mate.' It was Davey, his face trembling with emotion. The two men hugged.

Beside him, Serena was wiping tears from her eyes. 'I knew you'd make me cry.'

Pulling her closer, Arlo kissed her forehead softly. 'Then you can tick that off the list.'

Serena was a legendary list-maker—particularly when it came to organising events.

'Now, go and enjoy your party. Take Davey out on the dance floor. That'll put a smile back on your face.'

'Great speech.'

It was Frankie. The relief he'd felt moments earlier faded as he looked into her eyes. She looked happier than he'd ever seen her, and somehow sadder too.

'Thank you.'

She hesitated, seemingly on the point of saying something, and then changed her mind. He felt a sudden, overwhelming urge to hold her close, to steady his body against hers. Maybe that would stop this feeling of everything slipping beneath his feet.

'Would you dance with me?' he asked abruptly.

Her eyes found his and she nodded slowly. Taking her hand, he led her onto the dance floor. He held her close, letting the scent and the softness of her skin envelop him, so that by the end of their second dance his body was rock-hard.

She felt it. Of course she did. And, watching her blue eyes widen and flare, he leaned forward and nipped the soft skin of her throat.

'Can we go upstairs?' she whispered. 'I need you now.'

He didn't bother to answer. Instead, he took her hand and led her off the dance floor. He was dimly aware of people's faces. Dimly aware that their hunger must be visible to anyone looking. But all he cared about was getting across the ballroom and up to their bedroom as quickly as possible.

This was what he wanted—what they both wanted. It was all they needed from one another.

As they stepped out into the hall she tugged at his arm. 'Are you sure you want to leave?'

'I've never been more sure of anything,' he said hoarsely and, sweeping her into his arms, he carried her up the stairs.

When they reached the bedroom door his body was straining for release and, kicking it shut, he loosened his grip, bringing his mouth down on hers as her hands locked in his shirt and she dragged him towards her.

Tightening his arm around her waist, he pushed her back against the door, flattening her body with his. Her fingers were tugging at his waistband and he almost lost his footing as she pulled him free of his trousers and gripped him in her hand, and then he was lifting her and jerking up her dress in one swift movement.

She shifted against him as he yanked aside her panties and, breathing raggedly, thrust inside her. Opening her mouth to the heat of his kiss, she wrapped her legs around his waist, arching against him, panting out his name as he surged into her with hot, liquid force.

Frankie lifted the shotgun, her heart pounding as she closed her right eye and tried to visualise the path of the clay. It was easy to pick up the basics of shooting, Arlo had told her. But actually to hit the target...

'Weight on your front foot, bend your knee, stick out your bottom, fire when it's almost at the top of the curve...' she muttered to herself, and then, 'Pull!' she shouted.

The tiny disc spun into the air and—*bang!*—disintegrated with a satisfying crack.

Grinning idiotically, she turned to where Arlo and Davey stood watching her. 'I did it!'

'Well done,' said Arlo softly.

Holding the gun upright, she flicked the bolt so the gun broke. 'I did everything you said and it worked. It actually worked.'

He held her gaze. 'Yes, it did.'

She did a little dance on the spot. 'I didn't think I'd enjoy it that much, but it's so satisfying.'

Arlo grinned. 'My turn.'

Frankie watched dry-mouthed as he walked away. He had an enviable air of calm that made it seem as if he was moving at a slower pace than everyone around him. But then he tucked the gun into his shoulder and she felt suddenly weak in the middle as both his body and gun swiftly followed the four clays through the air with smooth, lethal accuracy.

She sighed. 'Has he always been like this? You know...'

'I do—and, yes. He's one of a kind.' Davey smiled. 'Last night he was being generous. He's the one who makes everything look easy.'

He did, Frankie thought, picturing Arlo giving his speech. Look at how he had just stood up in front of all those people and said those beautiful things about Davey and Serena. *And love.*

Her heart skipped a beat.

He had sounded so genuine.

But then he was hardly going to say what he really thought.

She knew that he didn't believe one word of it. He couldn't have made it clearer that he had given up on love. Only hearing him talk like that made it hard not to wish that he hadn't.

But only for a moment.

She felt a faint flush of heat wash over her cheekbones, remembering how he had carried her upstairs last night. She didn't need to complicate what was already perfect.

'So tell me? Did you have a good time last night?'

Serena gave her a one-armed hug. They were back at the house, where Serena had laid on a mouth-watering brunch.

'It was better than good.' Frankie smiled. 'It was the best party I've ever been to.'

She had really enjoyed herself—and yet, truthfully, she had preferred lunch yesterday, when it had been just the four of them. In fact, what she liked best of all was just lying on the sofa with Arlo in the library at the Hall...

Now that she thought about it, she'd only really started going out a lot at secondary school—and mostly that had been a kind of pushback against Harry and Amelie's glittering success.

And after the accident, her partying had been a way to fight the loneliness and the guilt and had ended up being her career. Now she couldn't imagine living like that. Only she was going to have to return—and sooner rather than later.

Blanking her mind to that unwelcome thought, she said quickly, 'I had a great time at the shoot as well.'

'I'm sorry I couldn't come down, but Bertie had me up before dawn with his teeth.'

Frankie glanced over at the small blond boy clutching at Serena. She had met Bertie yesterday, and he had been like a jumping jack. Now, though, there were smudges under his eyes and he seemed listless and quiet.

'Would you like me to take him for you?' Frankie asked as Serena attempted to pick up her coffee cup.

Stifling a yawn, Serena shook her head. 'He won't go to anyone when he's feeling like this—'

'Except his favourite godfather!'

Watching Bertie's face split into a huge, gap-toothed smile, Frankie felt a sharp nip of pleasure as Arlo reached forward and lifted him into his arms.

'I'm just going to grab some food,' he said, leaning in to kiss Serena on both cheeks. 'Do either of you want anything?'

Serena shuddered. 'No, thank you. I can still taste that last tequila.'

Arlo made a tutting sound. 'Frankie? Any preferences?'

'Surprise me,' she said softly.

His gaze locked with hers and she felt the air between them snap like an elastic band.

'I'll do my best.'

Watching him walk away, Serena sighed. 'He's so good with Bertie. I suppose he would be—I mean, he practically raised Johnny by himself.' She rested her elbows on the tablecloth. 'But never mind that now. What I want to know is how did you two meet?'

Frankie felt her mouth open and close as she tried to remember what she and Arlo had agreed, but before she could answer Serena waved her hands excitedly.

'No—no, wait a minute. Let me guess. Your car got a puncture and he pulled over to help? Or maybe you were lost—?'

'No, it was nothing like that.' Frankie shook her head. 'I know Johnny from London, and he introduced me to Arlo.' *That was almost true.* 'We hit it off and he asked me to stay.' *That was also almost true.*

To her astonishment, Serena looked delighted. 'Oh, I'm so happy you said that. It sounds so normal. I *knew* you were different from the others,' she said triumphantly.

The others.

Frankie felt something twist beneath her ribs. Not that long ago she'd found it hard to imagine anyone wanting to work with Arlo, let alone share his bed. Now, though, it hurt to imagine his body overlapping another woman's...

Leaning in conspiratorially, Serena lowered her voice. 'I was watching the two of you together and you can't keep your eyes off each other. I told Davey you must be the one—'

What? She stared up at Serena in shock and confusion. 'No, no... I don't think... That's not...'

Serena touched her hand. 'It's okay. I'm not going to say anything. I know Arlo's a very private person,' she said gently. 'But I know love when I see it.'

Love? No, that was wrong. That wasn't what was happening here. She and Arlo didn't love one another.

Her head started to spin. Around her, the room seemed to be blurring at the edges.

No, they didn't.

But she loved him.

She felt a rush of panic and confusion, then denial. That couldn't be true. It just couldn't. Surely you couldn't fall in love so quickly. But she knew that it was true. She *loved* him. Loved him with every frantic beat of her heart.

Her breath caught. But if that was true...

Gazing across the table at Serena, she felt her throat contract. She seemed so certain, and she and Davey knew Arlo better than anyone. But could Serena be right? Could Arlo have fallen in love with her too?

That question kept popping into her head during the rest of the day, but thinking it was one thing. Asking it...

Part of her wanted to. Another part—the part that didn't want to rock the boat—feared the consequences of demanding more when everything was going so well, and she was still dithering later that day, as the Rolls-Royce convertible rumbled back over the wet cobbles on the causeway.

'So, do you want to eat something?' he asked.

'I don't think so.' She thought for a moment. 'Actually, what I'd really like is a bath.'

Dipping his head, he kissed her softly on the mouth. 'Great minds think alike.'

It was lovely to have so much endless and guilt-free hot water on tap, Frankie thought as she lay back in the water, gazing through the spirals of steam to where Arlo lounged, his arms resting along the rim of the bath.

Looking at the heavy muscles bunching, she felt her pulse accelerate. It had always been easy to admire his solidness. But now she found it just as easy to admit that she loved everything about him that wasn't visible. In fact, she loved everything about him.

Only now that it was easy to admit that to herself, she could feel herself wanting to tell Arlo.

Striving for calm, she picked up the soap and began rubbing it between her hands. 'Thank you for taking me to Stanhope Park. I had a really nice time.'

'Well, you were a huge hit. Davey thinks you're wonderful, and Serena is raving about you too. They've invited us over on Saturday for lunch.'

His grey eyes rested on her face and, thinking back to her conversation with Serena, Frankie felt her stomach flip over. 'They're both lovely. And they loved your speech.' She hesitated. 'I loved it too. I thought it was beautiful. But—'

He stared at her steadily. 'But what?'

'I don't know how you could say all that stuff about love and not want it for yourself.'

Sitting forward, he scooped up some water and dribbled it over her bare breasts.

'I thought we'd talked about that,' he said after a long silence.

'We talked about your parents. But how do you know it would be the same for you? I mean it's not the same for Davey and Serena, and if you met your "for ever" person everything might feel different.'

His face stilled and she felt her heart start to thud against her ribs.

'I'm not the marrying kind—'

'How do you know? How *can* you know? You've never been married.' Her fingers bit into the soap. 'You talk about data and facts, but you're not basing your opinion on fact.'

There was another immeasurably long pause, and then he said coolly, 'Actually, that's exactly what I'm doing. You see, I have been married.'

She stared at him, mute with shock.

When? For how long? Who was she?

He flicked her a glance, hearing her questions even though she hadn't asked them. 'Ten years ago, for just under three months. Her name was Harriet and she was someone I met at university.'

Her heart was still thumping and she counted

the thuds, trying to steady herself. 'What happened?'

'I didn't love her. I told her. She left. It was not my finest moment.' His face was bleak. 'I wanted to love her. I wanted to have what my parents had. I wanted to believe. But it was a disaster. All I did was end up hurting her.' Reaching out, he prised the soap from her fingers, his hands covering hers. 'And that's why we can never be more than this. I don't want to hurt you, Frankie. I can't risk that.'

Her eyes were stinging but she made no move to touch them. There was nothing she could do. The flat, uncompromising edge in his voice left her nowhere to go.

'So what are you saying?' she said stiffly.

'I suppose I'm saying…is this enough for you?' His jaw was locked tight, the skin stretched taut across his cheekbones, and she could hear him breathing.

No, it wasn't.

She felt so much…wanted so much more.

She was on the verge of taking his hand and pressing it to her lips, telling him that she loved him. And she might have done it if he hadn't just told her what had happened with Harriet. But she couldn't unknow what she knew…couldn't unsee the weariness in his eyes…and she couldn't bring herself to tell him the truth.

Not now.

Not if it might mean losing this…losing him…

That was a risk she couldn't take.

She nodded slowly, her stomach lurching at the lie. 'Yes, it is.'

His face relaxed a little and she leaned forward and kissed him softly. She felt his hand touch her cheek and he deepened the kiss, and then she was kissing him back and surrendering to the tide of hunger rising inside her, letting it sweep aside her pain and her love.

CHAPTER TEN

THE NEXT MORNING they woke late. After days of bright sunshine the weather had turned and it was raining again. Not the deluge of last week, but enough for them to retreat to the library after a long, leisurely breakfast.

Now they were sprawled against each other on the rug in front of the fire. Frankie's head was in his lap, his hand was in her hair, and they were watching the flames as they curled sinuously over the logs.

Correction: Frankie was watching the flames.

He was watching her.

A couple of days ago at the party he'd thought she could never look any more beautiful, but he'd been wrong. Today, wearing jeans and some old jumper of his, with no make-up and her hair curling loosely over her shoulders, there was a kind of radiance about her that had nothing to do with the symmetry of her features or the luminous clarity of her skin.

It was about who she was as a person. And Frankie was a beautiful person.

His ribs tightened as he remembered the hours running up to the party.

To say that he'd been dreading it was an understatement. Being surrounded by his family was just so difficult, so painful. It stirred so many beautiful, precious memories, and it hurt to remember all that he had lost.

At three-line whip events—the ones he couldn't legitimately avoid—he usually just watched from the sidelines and left as early as possible. But Frankie had drawn him in, made him a part of every conversation, so that instead of brooding on the past, thinking of what he'd lost, he had found himself talking—not expansively, maybe, but talking just the same—and it had been fun.

She had made it fun.

She was so full of energy and curiosity about life, about people. He loved that about her.

To an outsider, his family might appear insular and cliquey and a little bit clueless about how the rest of the world lived. And they all knew each other. It would be daunting for anyone to be parachuted into such an environment, and he knew how nervous she had been.

But not one person there would have guessed. She had talked to everyone, laughed at Arthur's terrible jokes, and listened patiently while Davey explained the intricacies of his new biomass boiler.

She drew people out of themselves—and drew them together. Not in some stage-managed, artificial way, but naturally.

No wonder everyone had loved her.

And she had loved them.

His heart felt suddenly heavy inside his chest as he remembered the dazzle of happiness and excitement in her blue eyes. She had loved being a part of a family again, and he had loved being able to gift her that.

He felt his shoulders tense. That, though, was all he could give her.

What stopped him going further—what made it impossible for him even to indulge in thinking about going further—was Frankie herself.

She needed more than he could give. No, it was more than that. She needed more than he'd *shown* her he could give.

Talking to her last night in the bath, he'd made it sound as if hurting her was a risk. But 'risk' implied that there was another option where he *didn't* end up hurting her, and that wasn't true.

Memories of his short, unhappy marriage stirred and shivered inside his head.

Had he felt this way with Harriet?

Definitely not. He'd been too young, too desperate.

This time, though, he had no excuse to ruin a young woman's life.

And Frankie deserved better. After everything she'd already been through, she needed someone who could complete her life, not cause it to unravel.

His chest tightened.

And yet he couldn't seem to stop himself from

wanting to rearrange the world so that it would offer up a space where he and Frankie could be together. Although at the same time he needed it not to involve any kind of contract or commitment that could be broken.

In other words, he wanted something that didn't exist. Only he didn't have the first idea how to explain any of that to Frankie—which was why he'd ended up telling her about Harriet.

He'd never had to do that before. In the past, with other women, he'd found it easy to stick to his rules without needing to justify or explain himself. But right from the start Frankie had been different. Somehow she had sneaked under the tripwire, and before he had known what was happening she'd upended everything that had previously seemed so certain and inviolable.

Yesterday, she'd left him with no option. He'd had to tell her about his marriage to prove to her once and for all that it didn't matter what worked for other people. It hadn't worked for him.

'What is it?'

Frankie was looking up at him. She felt soft and warm against him, but it was the questioning look in her blue eyes that made his fingers still against her hair.

'Nothing.' He forced a smile as her gaze travelled over his face.

He had to stop this pointless back and forth. It was like trying to move forward in a whiteout.

But probably he was only feeling this way because he'd churned up the past, muddying the waters of the present.

'I was just thinking about maybe going for a dip.'

'You mean, in the sea?'

She wriggled upright, her eyes bright with the adventure of it. Leaning forward, she looped her hands around his neck so that he could feel the tips of her small pointed breasts against his chest.

'But won't it be freezing?'

'It'll be bracing.' He smiled. 'Don't worry. I'm not expecting you to come with me.'

She frowned. 'But I want to. Unless you're planning on swimming around the island or to Denmark?'

It hadn't occurred to him that she would want to join him. He thought she'd opt to stay by the fire. But now, gazing down at her eager face, it seemed blindingly obvious she would never do that.

He shook his head. 'I wasn't planning on being in for more than a couple of minutes,' he lied.

He'd actually been planning on swimming up to the rocks. But he was used to swimming in chilly seas. Frankie wasn't. And without a wetsuit it would be just too dangerous for her to do anything more than take a quick dip.

'Did you bring a costume with you?' he asked.

She nodded. 'I did.' Her mouth twitched. 'Why? Are you saying I don't need one?'

Their eyes met and he felt tiny curls of heat break like waves over his skin as he imagined Frankie coming naked out of the sea like Botticelli's *Venus*.

Feeling his body harden, he shook his head again. 'No, I'm not,' he said firmly, tipping her gently off his lap.

Another second of this and he would be in danger of losing both the power of speech and any desire to move. What he needed right now was to clear his head—and that wasn't going to happen when the soft press of Frankie's body was playing havoc with all his senses, including his common sense.

'Come on.' He held out his hand. 'Let's go and get changed—before I change my mind or you change it for me.'

The sea was glorious. Just how he liked it. The water was drawing up lazily and then hurling itself against the stretch of golden sand like a steeplechaser clearing the final fence.

It was cold—bracingly so—but not enough to stop Frankie from joining him with a shriek as the surging waves sloshed against her body.

They spent a few minutes plunging through the water and then, hand in hand, made their way back to the beach. Grabbing towels, they ran, shivering, up to the Hall.

'Not too hot to start,' Arlo warned her as she

unwrapped her body from its crimson swimsuit and stepped into the shower.

As she tilted her head back he joined her, gasping as the water hit his skin. Leaning forward, he let the warm stream soak his hair before smoothing it back against his skull.

Once they were done, and had stepped onto the tiled floor, he wrapped one of the huge plush towels around her and another round his waist, then pulled her closer, fitting her body snugly against his.

'Are you warm enough?' he asked.

Tipping her head back, she nodded. 'I should probably dry my hair...'

'Let me.'

He grabbed another towel and led her into the bedroom. The fire had been lit earlier, but it had died down, so he tossed another log into the gleaming orange core.

Turning, he felt his body harden. Frankie was sitting on the end of the bed, gazing up at him, her hair curling damply over her shoulders. She had let the towel fall away from her body, exposing the slim curves of her breasts, and he watched, mesmerised, as a droplet of water trickled all the way to the tip of her right nipple.

When she looked up at him, he reached down and began rubbing her soaked hair.

'That was fun.' She smiled. 'I thought the sea would actually be colder.'

'You're lucky. It's usually coldest in April.'

Their eyes met, and there were two, maybe three beats of silence. Then she reached up and pressed her hand against the front of his towel.

'That's not the only reason I'm lucky,' she said softly.

Abruptly, his body redirected the flow of his blood with such force that he had to put his hand against her shoulder to steady himself. His mouth dried and he was suddenly conscious of the hammering of his heart as she peeled the towel away from his body and let it slip onto the rug.

There was another beat of silence and then she wrapped one hand around his hard length, cradling him underneath with the other. Without releasing her grip, she pushed him back onto the bed, slipping between his legs as he shifted backwards. He breathed in sharply as she began stroking the taut, silken skin, moving his hand to grip her hair as she flicked her tongue over the blunted head of his erection.

Her hands found his thighs, her fingers splaying against the muscle, and he groaned with helpless pleasure as she took him deeper into her mouth, then deeper still, so that he was powerless to move.

Only he wanted to taste her too. To give her pleasure. Not out of obligation, or a need to prove his virility, but because her pleasure was essential to his enjoyment.

Tugging on her shoulders, he pushed her gently backwards and sat up, his mouth finding hers. He'd lost count of how many times they had kissed before, but as he felt her hands touch his face his heart began to race.

Her fingers were so light, so gentle. *So loving*.

Gritting his teeth, he fought against the sudden tenderness and, tearing his mouth away, pulled at her hips, kissing her stomach as he turned her body so that she was above his face.

His head was swimming. Breathing in her scent, he parted her damp flesh, dipping inside her, seeking the tight bud of her clitoris. Teasing her with his tongue, he felt her quiver, and she arched against his mouth, moaning.

'No, no—'

He felt her jerk backwards.

'I need you inside me.'

The hoarseness of her voice made him move more than the words she'd said.

Lifting her gently, he tried to pull her round to face him, only his leg got in the way. It would have been awkward if it had happened the first time, but they had nothing to prove now, he realised, and when she started to laugh it was the most natural thing in the world to bury his face in her hair and laugh too.

She sat up. 'Sorry, I didn't mean to kill the mood.'

'You haven't.'

She was straddling him, with his erection pressing against the slick heat between her thighs, and he couldn't remember ever feeling such an ache of longing. It went beyond want. This was need. A vast, untapped seam of need that was infinitely more powerful than desire.

His stomach tightened and, reaching up, he cupped her breasts, his thumbs grazing the nipples. 'I don't think anything could do that,' he said slowly. 'I want you all the time, Frankie.'

His hunger was like a burn, or an itch beneath the skin that no amount of scratching could satisfy. Her touch did something to him...made him want more and more.

'I want you too. I want you so much.' She sucked in a breath, her voice suddenly scratchy with emotion. 'I want—'

'Shh, Frankie, shh...' He placed his finger against her lips. 'It's okay, it's okay,' he said soothingly.

But, her eyes were so blue, so clear—too clear. He felt as if he could see into her soul, feel what she was feeling vibrating in his chest.

Only the fact that he was feeling anything other than desire was wrong. He didn't do feelings. That was why he couldn't offer her a real relationship— why this could only ever be about sex.

Heart hammering, unable to face the emotion in her eyes, he raised himself onto his elbows and kissed her desperately, passionately, fiercely, needing to wipe out the emotion churning inside him.

Pulse throbbing, he cupped her buttocks, taking her weight in his hands as she lowered herself onto him.

He gripped her hips and began to move slowly, wanting to take his time, to give her pleasure that would eclipse any he'd ever given her before.

His hands found her nipples and he tugged them gently, squeezing the taut tips, feeling a hot rush of satisfaction as a sound that quivered with pure sexual need broke from her lips.

Dropping his hands to her belly, he stroked the smooth skin and then, as she started to rock against him, slid his fingers between her thighs.

Her hands caught his wrists and, looking up at her face, he felt his body tighten so swiftly and strongly that he was afraid he would come there and then.

His body shuddered. *Yes*. This was what he wanted: heat and frenzy and release.

Blood roaring in his ears, he reached up and kissed her again, his fingers tightening in her hair as he felt his muscles start to tense, his own wave of pleasure building inside him, rising up, dark and unstoppable.

He felt her body lock around his as she cried out against his mouth, and then the wave hit him with full force, curling over him and pounding through him as he thrust into her.

Heart raging, he wrapped his arms around her body and buried his face in her hair. 'Frankie—'

Breathing out, he stroked a tangle of curls away from her face. His body was aching, almost hurting from the intensity of his orgasm, but then his eyes met hers, and the depth of emotion he saw there blotted out that pain with another kind of pain that made him look away.

His ribs felt too tight.

He didn't want to see that softness for him there. That was a need he couldn't meet. He'd tried once before, and failed, and nothing had changed.

He hadn't changed.

He might not be young and naive anymore, but he was still that same man. Still intense and unapproachable, uncommunicative and uncompromising. A man defined by his limits.

He could never be full of fire and drama like his father, or vivacious and beautiful like his mother and Johnny.

Out on the huge expanses of polar ice he was a hero. Here in the real world he felt awkward and inelegant. The idea of someone like him with a woman like Frankie was not just stupid, it was absurd. He might as well try and capture a flame in his hand.

Only last night, for the first time in his entire life, he had felt as if he was standing in the flames with Frankie.

He knew that it had never been like this with any other woman. Never been so easy, so intimate. *So personal.* But then before it had never mattered who he was with. This time it was all about Frankie.

'Hey,' he said softly, seeing her faraway expression. 'Where have you gone?'

She smiled. 'No, I'm here. I was just thinking…'

He was torn, caught between the need to know more and the fear of what he might hear.

'About what?'

'I was just thinking how strange time is when I'm with you. Sometimes it seems to stretch on for ever, and then other times it feels like everything has sped up.' She bit into her lip. 'Does that sound stupid?'

Staring at her steadily, he shook his head. 'When I'm with you everything feels so much sharper. Colours, sounds…'

There was a glow to her now, like the halo of light around the sun, and it would be so easy in the post-coital haze of intimacy and tenderness to step into that light.

He tilted her face, and the fragility of her neck and the delicate bones of her shoulders felt like a warning—a reminder of how easy it would be to hurt her by promising something he couldn't give.

So there would be no *Perhaps if…* or *Maybe some day…*

But he could be honest. He wanted to be honest.

His thumb stroked the upper bow of her mouth as he looked into her eyes. 'It's not been like that with other people. It's never been like this for me before.'

She breathed out shakily. 'Me neither.'

'But it works, doesn't it?'

Her expression was hazy, and then she nodded, and he knew that she was everything he wanted in the world right now.

And then he was pulling her closer, telling himself that when the time came he would let her go without a backward glance.

It was the only way.

They were eating lunch in the kitchen. Frankie was telling Constance about her dip in the sea, and he was half listening, half watching the play of emotions over her face, when he felt his phone vibrate in his pocket.

Since that day on the beach, when Frankie had told him about the accident, he'd left it on silent, and he was all ready to ignore it until he saw the name on the screen.

Johnny.

'I'm just going to get this,' he said and, pushing his chair back from the table, stood up and walked out into the hallway.

'Arlo.'

At the sound of Johnny's voice he felt a rush of relief fill his chest. Like most siblings, he knew the tell-tale signs of distress in his brother, but there was no breathless note of panic.

'Hey, little brother. Nice of you to get in touch.'

Johnny groaned. 'I know… I know. I'm useless. I really was going to call—'

The line was so clear that if he closed his eyes it would be as if Johnny was standing beside him, and he felt a sharp stab of longing to reach out and hug his brother.

'It's just been completely mad. Honestly, Hollywood people are crazy.'

Suddenly Johnny's voice sounded muffled, and Arlo could almost picture him, head bent over his phone conspiratorially.

'They never seem to sleep. It's like there's no difference between day and night. They just keep on going.' He laughed. 'You'd fit right in.'

Arlo felt his heart contract with love. Hollywood was the last place on earth he'd fit in, but his brother's partisan adoration knew no limits.

'On that basis, so would about twelve million penguins.'

Johnny laughed again. 'True.' There was a pause, then, 'I'm really sorry I haven't called.'

'It's okay. I know you're busy—'

'So are you. And that's one of the reasons I wanted to call. To thank you for letting Frankie stay at the Hall.'

Arlo felt his chest tighten. 'You don't have to thank me, Johnny, it's your home too.'

'I know. But I also know how busy you are, and you weren't expecting her...' He paused again, then, 'So has it been okay?'

'Of course.' It was suddenly hard to speak. To find words that could describe how 'okay' it had been. 'It was Davey and Serena's anniversary party, so we went over to Stanhope, and she's helped me with some of my notes. Oh, and she's trounced me at billiards.'

He heard his brother chuckle. 'Yeah, she's pretty good, isn't she?' There was another pause. Then, 'I'm glad she's had some fun. That's actually the other reason I'm calling.'

Arlo frowned. 'What is?'

'I wanted to do something to make up for letting her down, so I've bought her a ticket to LA.'

His head felt as if it was not connected to his body. 'A ticket?' he asked slowly.

'Yeah, for Saturday. It's a surprise. I thought she could do with a few days in the sun and I think she'll adore LA. It's got everything she loves. Sandy beaches, shopping malls. *And celebrities!* I mean, Frankie was made for this place.'

No, she wasn't, he thought, his forehead creasing into a frown. Frankie was made for family brunches and swimming in the sea.

Arlo stared across the beautiful empty hallway, listening to his brother's voice, feeling a dark, heavy cloud swelling inside his chest.

What was it he'd said earlier to Frankie about their 'arrangement'?

It works, doesn't it?

He felt his whole body tense with fury and disgust. What the hell had he been thinking? Did he really think that was all she deserved? Some open-ended affair with a man who could essentially offer nothing more than sex and his own shortcomings?

She needed sunshine and cocktails and people her own age—like Johnny.

He cleared his throat, making his voice level. 'It sounds like you want her to stay for more than a few days.'

'Yeah, I do.' Johnny hesitated. 'She could really make a go of it out here, Arlo. She's got something about her... I think everyone is going to love her.'

Of course they would, Arlo thought, his fingers tightening around the phone.

The anonymous ache in his chest was no longer nameless. Only it had taken the thought of losing her for him to understand what it was. To understand that it was love.

His heart felt as if it would burst.

He loved her.

And he knew that Frankie loved him. She was too scared to say it out loud, but earlier, upstairs in the bedroom, he had felt it in every touch and kiss.

So what was he waiting for?

Hang up the phone. Go and tell her.

He felt euphoric, adrift with love. The need to find her and declare his feelings rose up inside him and he half turned, his body filling with lightness.

And then he stopped.

He couldn't do it.

He couldn't do that to Frankie—not if he loved her.

Suddenly he was terrified, almost breathless

with the fear that he would give in. Terrified of what would happen if he did.

Because he knew what would happen.

He knew Frankie.

She would leap wholeheartedly, loving him, trusting him to catch her...

But her trust would be misplaced. He couldn't trust himself not to fail, and if he failed he would hurt her more than he was already going to have to hurt her. And he *was* going to hurt her. It was the only way, even though the thought of doing so tore his heart in two.

'Would you like another cup of coffee?'

Glancing up at Constance, Frankie shook her head. 'I'm fine. But could you leave the pot?'

Arlo would want one. When he returned. She glanced over at the doorway, wondering who had called him. Not work. He would have ignored it.

He *had* ignored it—for her.

Her heart squeezed. He had put his life on hold for her and showed her how to live again. He had held her and comforted her and filled her with his strength—metaphorically and literally.

Look at this morning. Arlo had still been inside her, his arms anchoring her to his body, and her love for him had been so complete, so devastating, that the room had started to spin and she hadn't been able to see him clearly.

Not that it mattered. He was so familiar to her

now that even if she closed her eyes she could see every minute detail of his appearance.

Her fingers trembled against the handle of her coffee cup. He was so beautiful, and the lines on his face and the scars all over his body didn't diminish that beauty—they just made his beauty unique. More than unique. It was essential. He was essential to her now. She needed him more than she needed her next breath. He was everything. Her always and her for ever.

Only she couldn't tell Arlo that.

That wasn't what he'd signed up for and no alteration in her feelings could change that. She was already out of her depth, but at least there was still a way back to shore. She couldn't allow herself to get in any deeper. She couldn't let herself care even more for Arlo than she did. Not when she knew what it felt like to lose someone you loved. She couldn't go through that again.

Her pulse skipped. And she didn't need to. He had acknowledged that what they shared was different...special.

'It's never been like this for me before.'

Those had been his exact words, and right now that was enough.

'Anyway, I'll talk to you soon.'

She glanced up. It was Arlo. He was still on the phone, and as she looked at him, he pointed at it.

'Yes, I'll hand you over to her now.' He held out his phone. 'It's Johnny. He wants to talk to you.'

'Johnny—oh, my goodness! How's it going? I can't believe you're actually going to be in a *film*!' she gushed.

Johnny laughed. 'Don't blink or you'll miss me. I think one of the palm trees is on screen longer than I am.'

It was strange, hearing his laugh. A week ago it would have left her feeling weak. Now, though, she felt nothing except a kind of sisterly affection.

'Are there really palm trees?' she asked quickly.

She didn't care if there were or not, but she could feel Arlo's eyes on her face and felt suddenly self-conscious.

'Loads. Would you like to see them?'

'Of course.' She was momentarily distracted as, smiling stiffly, Arlo got up and walked over to the window.

'You would? Because that's why I'm calling. I've bought you a ticket to LA. You'll fly out on Saturday.'

She blinked. *But Arlo wasn't in LA.*

'Frankie! Are you still there? Did you hear what I said?'

'Yes, I did. That's amazing.' She forced a note of excitement into her voice. 'But you shouldn't have—'

'Yes, I should,' he said firmly. 'And Arlo thinks so too.'

'He does?' Her heart began hammering inside her chest.

'Yeah, he thinks you need a proper holiday. And besides, he's going to be in Svalbard at the end of the month.'

Her stomach felt as if it was filled with ice. She felt stunned, stupid, small.

Turning her head, she stared across the room to where Arlo was gazing at the sea. There was tension in his body and she knew he was seeing a different blue sea—one dotted with sharp-toothed icebergs.

'It's addictive,' he'd said.

She'd thought he'd been talking figuratively. But how could she compete with such beauty and majesty?

'Look, I know it's short notice, Frankie, but I also know I let you down.'

Johnny's voice broke into her thoughts and she gazed down into her cooling cup of coffee. 'It doesn't matter,' she said quietly.

'It does to me. So please let me make it up to you. Come to LA.'

She sucked in a steadying breath. 'I'd love to.'

As she hung up Arlo turned to face her, and the cool distance in his eyes left her in no doubt as to how he was really feeling.

In his head, he was already there on the ice. Maybe he'd never left. No wonder he couldn't promise anything in the way of commitment.

'So you're off to LA.'

It was a statement, not a question, but she still nodded.

'It's for the best, Frankie.'

'For whom?' She stood up abruptly and walked towards him.

'For you, of course. You're twenty-one. You have your whole life ahead of you, and that life isn't going to start here—'

With me.

He didn't say those words, but they both heard them. But he hadn't heard what *she* had to say. What she needed him to hear...to know.

She was done with hiding the truth. It hadn't stopped her losing everyone she loved and needed before, but it might stop her losing the man she loved and needed now.

She moved to his side. 'But what if I told you I loved you? Would that change anything?'

Only even before he shook his head, she knew that it wouldn't. That he already knew, and it didn't matter.

And knowing that he knew, and that it hadn't changed anything, gave her the strength to pull back and not leap unthinkingly with her eyes wide open.

It was over.

She couldn't do what she suspected Harriet had done—just hope that this difficult, conflicted man would change over time, for her. Maybe she might have done before the accident, but not now. Not knowing what she did about the agony of loss.

It was just so hard to let it go—to let *him* go.

'I don't want your love. And I don't want to hurt you. I want to be honest with you.' He glanced away from her. '*This*…what we had…was amazing. You're amazing.'

Had. There had been no moment of decision but already he was talking in the past tense, as if the choice had been made.

She stared at him in silence. 'Just not amazing enough,' she said slowly. She felt as if someone had punched her in the stomach, and her fingers curved protectively against the ache.

'No, that's not true.' His eyes narrowed on her face. 'This isn't about you.'

She stared at him, her heart breaking. 'You're right. It is about *us*. And I think you're not giving us a chance.'

Say something, she willed him. *Ask me not to go to LA.*

But a distance had opened between them now that seemed impossible to bridge and he said nothing.

Disbelief thudded inside her head.

After everything that had happened, surely it couldn't end like this?

As the silence lengthened, grew weighty, she could bear it no more. 'I don't think there's any point in me staying, so I'm going to go upstairs and pack. Can you call me a cab?'

'I'll take you to the station.' His voice was hard and flat.

Turning, she walked back across the kitchen, stopping in the doorway. 'You know, you saved me, Arlo—not just on the causeway, but here.' She touched her head. 'And here.' She touched her heart. 'You made me trust myself and I'll always be grateful.'

Her heart was aching, as if it had been torn in two, but she was going to leave nothing unsaid.

'I know that if anyone can save the world it's you. But I just hope that one day you meet someone who can rescue you.' She took a breath, pushing back against the pain of imagining that scenario. 'Someone who can make you trust in love again… make you trust yourself. Someone who will make you see that love is a risk worth taking and that a life without risks that aren't to do with cold and ice and danger is no life at all.'

There was nothing more to say. The weight of misery pressing against her heart was unbearable and, turning, she walked swiftly out of the room.

CHAPTER ELEVEN

THE TRAIN BURST out of the tunnel with a rush of warm air and a high-pitched squeal of brakes that filled the platform at Covent Garden underground station.

Frankie joined the crowd of commuters and shoppers jostling one another into the carriage. There was nowhere to sit so she grabbed hold of a hanging strap, leaning her head wearily into the crook of her elbow. She felt exhausted, although there was no real reason why she should. She'd hardly left the flat since getting back to London.

In fact, today was the first day she'd actually bothered to change out of her pyjamas, and it was a shock seeing herself reflected in the grimy window. A lot of the time over the last three days she had felt as if she was slowly being erased.

As the train started to judder forward she mechanically tightened her grip, shrinking into her coat. Her shoulders tensed. Even the thought that she might accidentally be thrown against someone made her feel queasy.

It wasn't personal.

Except it was.

She just couldn't bear the idea of touching someone who wasn't Arlo.

Or maybe it was the knowledge that she would never touch Arlo again that was making her feel so unsteady.

The train rumbled into the next station and she watched numbly as people got on and off, remembering those final few minutes they'd shared.

It had been almost a second-by-second replay of the first time he'd put her on a train. He had lifted her bag up onto the luggage rack and told her to have a good trip, and then turned and walked away.

Gazing at the window, she let her reflection blur. The difference was that Arlo hadn't come back for her. She had sat in the empty carriage, waiting, hoping, praying… But two minutes later the train had pulled out of the station.

In many ways it had been unremarkable—just a train leaving a station. To her, though, it had been as if day had turned into night.

Her eyes burned. She hadn't cried then. She still hadn't cried. The tears were there, but for some reason they wouldn't fall.

It was raining as she walked out of the tube station. It had been raining ever since she'd left Northumberland—a steady grey drizzle that made people hurry home.

Home.

Her throat tightened. It made no sense to think of the Hall as home, and yet it felt to her more like home than the flat.

Turning into the street where she lived, she plodded through the puddles uncaringly.

But, of course, home was where the heart was—and her heart was with Arlo...would always be with Arlo.

Only he didn't want her heart.

He couldn't have made that any plainer, but it had taken her until this morning to finally accept that as one of the unchangeable, absolute truths that Arlo so loved.

Her heart contracted. How long was this going to last? Her every thought beginning and ending with Arlo?

Glancing up, she felt her breath catch. A tall man was standing by her front door, face lowered, shoulders hunched against the rain.

Her feet stuttered and then she was stumbling forward, breaking into a run, a trace of hope working its way through her blood, flaring into the light.

'Arlo—'

He turned, and disappointment punched her in the diaphragm. It wasn't him.

'Thank goodness. I was worried you'd already left.'

It was her neighbour Graham. Beside him was a huge cardboard box.

'They tried to deliver this earlier, but you were out.'

She forced a smile. 'That's so kind of you, Gray, thank you.'

'No worries. Do you need me to take it inside?'

'No, it's fine. Honestly.'

He looked relieved. 'I'll see you when you get back, then. Have a good time.'

Upstairs in the flat, she dried her hair with a towel and frowned at the box. It was probably just some designer, sending her stuff to promote.

But when she tore off the parcel tape and stared down at the suitcase a lump built in her throat. She replayed the moment on the causeway when the wheel on her old suitcase had broken, snapping the thought off before she got to the part where Arlo had scooped her into his arms.

Because, of course, Arlo had sent the parcel. He had a pile of exactly the same suitcases in his bedroom.

There was an envelope with her name written on the front, and heart pounding, she opened it. Inside was a plain correspondence card, and written in Arlo's familiar slanting handwriting was a message.

I'm sorry.

The pain made breathing impossible. She curled over, clutching the card, and finally did what she had been unable to do for the last three days.

She wept.

'Come on, then.'

Patting the sofa, beside him, Arlo breathed out

unevenly as Nero jumped up onto the velvet cushions. He didn't normally let the lurcher up on the furniture, but there was something comforting about the dog's warm fur against his hand.

His throat tightened. Not that he deserved to be comforted after how he'd acted.

Picturing Frankie's stunned, pale face, he tensed his fingers against Nero's head. He had been so blazingly certain, so smugly convinced that he was in control...that he had got it all worked out.

Now all his assumptions seemed at best naive and at worst inhuman.

She had told him she loved him and the stark honesty of her words had unmanned him. Coward that he was, he had thought she would leave that unspoken, so that he could keep on pretending that he didn't know how she felt.

How *he* felt.

He gritted his teeth.

So many times out on the ice he had been faced with a crossroads—a moment in his journey when a decision had to be made. A choice that could mean either life or death. And each time he'd made a choice.

It was what he did. He spoke about it at schools. In lecture theatres at universities. The great explorer Arlo Milburn, talking about risk...about how every step in any direction was ultimately a leap of faith.

But he hadn't made that leap for Frankie. He

loved her and he had let her leave, and this time tomorrow she would be on her way to LA.

And in a week's time he would be out on the ice, living the life he'd told her he wanted. A life he had chosen over her. A life that suited someone like him—someone who found the prospect of having a woman who loved him too risky. A life where risk was confined to sub-zero temperatures and blizzards.

In other words, not a life worth living.

There. It was done. Finally she was packed.

Letting out a breath, Frankie got to her feet and stared down at her plush new suitcase. She had dithered about taking it, but in the end it had seemed churlish not to—and anyway her old suitcase was ruined.

She glanced at the clock by her bed. The taxi would be here in a minute, but that was fine. She just had to get her coat and then she would be ready to go.

She was going to get to the airport hours before she needed to, but that was what she'd decided to do last night, after she'd finally finished crying. She had cried a lot. About the accident and her family and about Arlo. At one point she had thought she might never stop crying, but at one minute past midnight she had run out of tears.

And that was when she'd made up her mind that today was going to be the first day of her new life.

Obviously, she wasn't going to just forget all her problems. But there was no future in living in the past and she wanted to start living again.

That was what Arlo had given her. He had helped her take that first step. More than anything she had wanted him to join her on the rest of her journey, only that wasn't to be.

But she wasn't just going to mark time and blog, like she had after the accident. She was going to go out into the world and live her life. Do some travelling. Make some new friends—real friends. Reconnect with old ones. Learn a new skill.

The intercom buzzed and, shrugging on her coat, she took the handle of her suitcase and glanced slowly around the flat. Maybe when she came back she would finally make this into a home.

She always used the famous black London cabs for work. The cabbies were always fun to talk to, and it looked cool arriving at events in one. Now, she found the familiar beetle shape of the car comforting.

As she buckled up, the cabbie turned round. 'It's Heathrow, isn't it?'

Frankie nodded. 'Yes, please.'

'Going somewhere nice, are you?'

'Los Angeles.'

'Lovely. Me and the wife went there last year. Then we did a road trip to New York.' He laughed. 'I know! I spend all day in the cab and then I do three weeks driving across America for my holidays. But I loved it. Every day felt like an adventure.'

Frankie smiled. 'This is a bit of an adventure for me too. My friend moved out there a few weeks ago and out of the blue he called up and invited me to stay.'

'Already? He's keen!'

'Oh, it's nothing like that. We're just friends.'

'Course you are.'

Looking up, she could see the cabbie grinning in the rear-view mirror.

'Just so you know, I'm going to shoot right at the traffic lights. I wouldn't normally, but there's roadworks on Woodley Road.'

She nodded. 'Okay.' Frowning, she pulled out her phone. 'Or you can try Mercer Street and then Warwick Park—'

Her voice stalled in her throat. The phone in her hand felt suddenly leaden. Or maybe that was her limbs.

Heart thumping, she stared down at the screen. She had been planning to check the route, but instead she was looking at the last journey she'd searched.

To Northumberland.

She'd thought she couldn't cry any more. But now tears started to roll down her cheeks.

Turning her head towards the window, she took a breath. The rows of terraced houses had given way to shops and banks and cafés. Already the streets were starting to buzz with life.

LA would be bigger, brighter, busier.

But it would still seem empty to her.

Everywhere would always be empty if Arlo wasn't there.

'No, no, no… Now, don't you go getting upset.'

Glancing into the mirror, Frankie saw that the cabbie was looking at her in horror.

'You don't need to worry,' he said. 'I know a detour that'll get you to the airport in plenty of time. You'll have your adventure, I promise.'

She felt her heartbeat accelerate.

Not if she went to the airport, she wouldn't.

Wiping her eyes, she leaned forward. 'Actually, we're going to have to take a slightly bigger detour…'

Arlo woke late on Saturday morning. He had been awake for most of the night, willing the morning to come so that he could get the day over and done.

He'd expected it to be grey and dull, but the weather forecasters had got it spectacularly wrong and after days of rain the skies had cleared and the sun was beaming above the horizon.

But it wasn't the sudden upturn in the weather that had got him out of bed.

It was Frankie.

His mouth twisted.

Only not quite Frankie.

She had been there in his dreams, and just as he'd begun to wake her soft body had pressed tightly against his. He had felt her warmth, and relief had spread through his limbs. And then he had woken properly, and her absence had been like a crushing weight on his chest, so that he'd had to get up and move about.

He should be packing. But that would mean going into his bedroom, and he had been avoiding it for days, choosing instead to sleep in one of the spare rooms.

Downstairs, the house was silent and still, and he made his way into the kitchen, Nero padding lightly after him. It would all be over soon. Just this last day to get through and then she would be gone. In a week he would join the expedition at Svalbard and lose himself in the fathomless expanse of the Arctic.

His phone rang, the noise jolting him, and he felt a sudden rush of raw, unfiltered hope. But as he glanced down at the screen it swiftly drained away.

He hesitated, debating how to swipe, and then he made up his mind. 'Davey. How are you?'

'Oh, I'm fine. But apparently you have lost your mind.'

Arlo frowned. He could count on the fingers of one hand the number of times he and Davey had fallen out, but on those rare occasions his cousin had always been placatory—apologetic, almost.

Now, though, his cousin's voice was shaking with either anger or frustration or both.

'What are you talking about?' he asked.

But he didn't need to ask the question. He already knew what—*who*—Davey was talking about.

'I'm talking about Frankie.'

Arlo felt his heart twist. Hearing her name out loud hurt more than he would have thought possible. Hearing it out loud seemed to make her absence more vivid, more real. *Too real*.

Rubbing his eyes with the heel of his hand, he said stiffly, 'I don't want to talk about Frankie—'

'Well, I do.' He heard Davey take a breath. 'Serena called her. Just to find out if she wanted to ride before lunch on Saturday. Apparently, she's going out to LA to see Johnny.'

Arlo swore silently. He'd forgotten all about lunch. 'I should have called. I'm sorry—'

'I don't care about lunch. *We* don't care about lunch. We care about you, and why you ended things with Frankie.'

'I didn't end anything,' he said flatly. 'It wasn't that kind of relationship.'

'What kind? You mean the kind where you can't take your eyes off one another?'

Arlo bent his head, struggling against the truth of Davey's words. 'Exactly. It was a physical thing, and it burned out.'

He had never lied to his cousin before, and the lie tasted bitter in his mouth.

There was a long silence, and then Davey said quietly, 'It didn't burn out. You snuffed it out. Like you always do. Only it never mattered before. But Frankie's different. She loves you—really loves you.'

'I know—' The words were torn from his mouth.

His heart contracted as he remembered the moment he'd given her the bracelet and how she'd been upset for giving him nothing in return.

She *had* given him something. She had given him her love and her trust. She was a gift—beautiful, unique, irreplaceable.

'And you love her.' The anger had faded from Davey's voice. 'I know you don't want to admit it, and I know why.'

Picturing the moment when he'd rejected Frankie, Arlo felt a pain sharper than any physical injury he'd ever endured. He had told her he wanted to be honest and then he had lied to her face.

'I can admit it, but it doesn't change anything. I tried marriage, commitment, love—whatever you want to call it.' His chest tightened, and remembered misery and panic reared up at him. 'It was a disaster.'

'Yes, it was. Because you were young and you were grieving and you made a mistake. And if you'd been like everyone else on the planet—like me and Johnny and Arthur—you would have known that was *all* it was.'

He heard Davey sigh.

'But you hadn't ever made a mistake. You were always so smart, and so in control, and you didn't like how it felt. And when you got divorced you didn't just walk away from Harriet. You walked away from love.'

Arlo felt his throat tighten. His eyes were burning. He hadn't walked. He had run. He had turned and run away from love and kept on running until some cosmic force had put Frankie in his path... or rather in his bed.

Frankie, with her fiery curls and freckles, her permafrost-melting smile and her teasing laughter, which trailed a promise of happiness like the tail of a kite high in the bluest sky.

More than anything he wanted to turn and follow her, but—

'I have to keep on walking because nothing's changed,' he said slowly.

He couldn't change his past.

Davey cleared his throat. 'Everything's changed. Frankie is not Harriet, for starters. But what's changed the most is you. You're different with her.'

Different *because* of her, Arlo thought, his fingers tightening around the phone.

'And you don't need me to tell you what to do. Just to tell you that it's not too late,' Davey said softly.

But Davey was wrong, he thought, his heart swelling against his ribs. It had been too late from the moment he first saw Frankie. All this panic and doubt was just him struggling to catch up with the truth.

For so long he'd been so fixed on the idea of absolutes that he'd been blind to the beautiful potential of a life where random events simply challenged you to take new directions. Like down a causeway in the middle of a storm. Or to a crowded family party.

He swallowed past the lump in his throat. 'Then I should probably get going if I'm going to stop Frankie catching that plane.'

Hanging up, he glanced at his watch. If he left now, he could catch her at the airport...

It took him less than ten minutes to grab his jacket, find the keys to the Rolls, and more or less run outside to where the huge gold car sat slumbering on the warm driveway.

His heart was leaping.

Three days ago the past—his and hers—had felt like insurmountable obstacles to a future where he and Frankie could be together. But she had been right. Love conquered everything, even the obstacles around his heart, and now nothing would stop them being together.

He knew now that he didn't need or want to chase what his parents had shared.

He wanted and needed Frankie.

Together, they would make a life that was rich and enticing and joyful—but not perfect. Why would he want perfect? It was their flaws, their failings, that had brought them together, and it was in failing that they'd found strength in themselves and one another.

Turning the car around, he began rumbling over the cobblestoned causeway, tensing his muscles to stop himself from just putting his foot down on the accelerator pedal and flooring it.

There was plenty of time.

He had a full tank of fuel so he would only need to stop once.

He frowned. *What was happening?* The steering wheel was turning in his hands like a dog pulling on its lead, and there was an ominous choking sound coming from the engine.

His hands clenched around the wheel, urging the big car on. But he could feel the power dying, and he watched as with slow, agonising inevitability the Rolls slid slowly to a standstill.

Switching off the engine, he yanked up the handbrake and threw himself out of the car. He flipped open the bonnet and stared down at the engine. He had no idea what was wrong with it. The alternator, maybe?

But that wasn't something he could fix right here and now. He needed another car.

He began to run back to the house. He would take the Land Rover.

His footsteps faltered. Except he couldn't. Constance had taken it to go shopping in Newcastle.

Even if he called her it would take her at least an hour and ten minutes to get back and that was too long.

The train would take even longer.

What he needed was a taxi—only of course there was no phone signal out here, and it would take him twenty minutes to run back to the house…

Heart hammering against his ribs, he squinted into the pale sunlight. He must be seeing things.

Except he wasn't.

There really was a London black cab rumbling slowly over the cobblestones.

It stopped in front of the Rolls and he stared in shock—not at the car, but at the woman stepping into the sunlight.

'Do you need some help?' she asked.

Frankie was standing there, her red hair gleaming in the sunlight.

'What are you doing here?'

He watched without blinking as she walked towards him, scared to blink in case she disappeared. His throat tightened with love and longing as she stopped in front of him.

'Oh, you know… I was in the area.'

'But you'll miss your flight.'

Frankie nodded. 'That's the plan. Although it only really became a plan this morning, when I was on my way to the airport.'

Arlo swallowed. His mouth was dry, and he felt breathless with shock and hope. 'I was on my way there too.'

Her face tensed. 'To go to Svalbard?'

'No.' He took a step forward. 'I'm not going to Svalbard. I was coming to find you. To stop you from leaving.'

She took a step forward too, and now he could see his love and longing reflected in her beautiful blue eyes.

'And why do you want to stop me from leaving?' she said shakily.

Lifting his hands, he cupped her face. 'Because I love you and I need you. And I want to spend my life with you.'

'You love me!' Frankie echoed, and then she started to cry. All the way up in the taxi she had been picturing Arlo's face, imagining what he might say, but the simple, absolute truth of his words were more than she could have wished for.

'I want to spend my life with you too. More than anything. I love you so much.'

'Not as much as I love you.'

His face creased and she saw that he was crying too.

'I can't believe that I let you go. Or that you came back—'

'Of course I came back. Everything else in my life is optional. But you—you're like air to me. I can't breathe without you.'

* * *

Arlo pulled her closer, his mouth finding hers. 'I can't breathe without you either.'

He could hardly believe what was happening. Not just that she was here, and that she loved him and he loved her, but that love had come so simply and completely.

'I made everything a struggle,' he said softly. 'I fought the past, my family, and most of all myself, because I was scared of being proved right. But I've never been happier to be proved wrong.'

He felt her hands slide around his body and they looked into each other's eyes, both of them certain that here in each other's arms they were in the right place—the only place they would ever want to be.

* * * * *

Enchanted by Beauty in the Billionaire's Bed?
Get wrapped up in these other
Louise Fuller stories!

Craving His Forbidden Innocent
The Terms of the Sicilian's Marriage
The Rules of His Baby Bargain
The Man She Should Have Married
Italian's Scandalous Marriage Plan

Available now!